BLACKEYES

ALSO BY DENNIS POTTER

Sufficient Carbohydrate
Waiting for the Boat: On Television
Ticket to Ride
The Singing Detective

BLACKEYES

DENNIS POTTER

VINTAGE BOOKS
A Division of Random House
NEW YORK

FIRST VINTAGE BOOKS EDITION, October 1988

Library of Congress Cataloging-in-Publication Data
Potter, Dennis.
Blackeyes.
I. Title.
PR6066.077B56 1988   823'.914   88-40204
ISBN 0-679-72047-2 (pbk.)

Manufactured in the United States of America

TO MY DAUGHTERS

1

The lovely Jessica sat alone at a small white table in front of a smaller white page, and although she looked so neat and demure there was murder in her heart. Her mind was puckering into the folds of a fierce concentration, but none of the tension which comes from hard and unfamiliar thinking had shown itself on the apparently calm oval of her face. The words would not come, as words will not when the task they are supposed to fulfil is beyond the reach of reason. She had learnt already that it was as difficult as it was tedious to try to describe the disturbing events in her own broken-into dreams, let alone the almost incomprehensible darkness in someone else's. But before the ink could flow, she needed to slither and splash into the rotting swamp behind the bony walls of the old man's head.

'Maurice James Kingsley', she intoned in a deliberately theatrical resonance, 'took it for granted that sleep and torment were natural partners, holding trembling hands in the endless mire.'

She continued to speak out loud for several minutes, and without hesitation, as though reciting menacing floridities that she had already written. Her long green eyes – once on the cover of many a magazine – swivelled to look at the movements of her mouth as it shone silkily scarlet in the mirror, long-stemmed and angled at the edge of the table.

'And every morning that he struggled awake in the unclean tangle of his bed,' she was saying, without the tiniest glint to acknowledge her excess, 'he failed to see the significance of the warnings which had been sent out from within his sleeping skull.'

The trouble was, the old man was much more likely to awaken these days to the vanilla tastes of sweet self-justification, or even triumph. His bed, so to speak, was full of laurel leaves, or adulatory newspaper cuttings.

The success of what was universally taken to be Maurice James Kingsley's final work of fiction had taken everyone by surprise, possibly including the seventy-seven-year-old author himself. He had, so far as was known, degenerated into a rather unsavoury eccentric with odd opinions, bizarre habits, and dated, almost *fin-de-siècle* mannerisms. A faded relic heavily reliant upon scrounging from his remaining few acquaintances and the necessarily meagre patronage of almost equally seedy producers nearly as old as himself at Broadcasting House, just around the corner from where he lived. He had not sunk so low as to have one of his now very occasional Occasional Pieces rejected by the *Spectator* or accepted by the *Daily Telegraph*, but there had been little hint that his dried-up old frame was going to produce such a late bloom.

Sugar Bush, as the book was called, had in fact lifted its title from a once popular song of South African origins which Kingsley long ago used to hum when in his cups. One of the reasons for the novel's success can perhaps be grasped by knowing that the old man had no idea that there was a nudging suggestion of obscenity about his title. The imagined allusion to female pubic hair had, in the publisher's phrase, done the novel no harm at all.

It told the story of a young model from her first audition to her final tragedy, a span of less than a decade. Later critics would come to see that the author had in truth made little attempt to give the unfortunate girl any sort of character or personality, but for the moment, at least, this sparseness was heralded as a fine example of an essential economy of art capable of bringing to life a touchingly enigmatic and elusive young woman.

Events in the narrative were rarely presented from her point of view, even though her especial claim to beauty was supposed to be the dark luminosity of her steady eyes. This had the effect of making her docility or sometimes astonishing passivity the central theme of the story. She was always present, always

2

absent. The actions and postures of those in the trade around her were thus thrown into a harsher light. What was still frequently thought of as glamorous or glitzy was revealed to be tawdry and venal: and yet the 'exposure' – for it was not entirely by design – remained ambivalent enough to catch the sparkle of the sequins and the gloss of the skin. Kingsley, by accident, was able to have his cake and eat it.

The reviewers, too, had come up trumps. It had been more than twenty years since Maurice James Kingsley had produced a novel, and time had gouged out a protective dike around him. His late bloom was greeted like a lost wild-flower miraculously surviving in a sprayed hedgerow. There are few things more likely to coax generosity out of British literary critics than such an opportunity to cloak their sentimentality, conservatism, and beleaguered nostalgia in the pleasures of the longer perspective. A crick in the neck from looking backwards was considered to be the sweetest of aches in these circles, especially when the work which causes it is the effort of a man who is so old that he can no longer be counted as a genuine rival.

The reaction of the predominantly middle aged and mostly male contingent of otherwise bored and exhausted reviewers was understandable. What was more surprising, perhaps, was the enthusiasm of much younger critics who had no need to call back yesterday, and sufficient juice in their loins not to get their sex out of a book as evasive as this one.

But the tenderfoot media stars saw many ironies in Kingsley's relaxed prose where few were actually intended. They insisted upon turning what was meant to be straightforward description into an elegantly glancing satire, and the author's peevish rancour into a cleansing anger. *Blitz* and *The Face* and *Time Out*, as well as *KRITZ*, went into those dyslexic paroxysms of enthusiasm by which the young and half-educated affect to celebrate the twilight of what they think of as the Western World and its consumer-based sexism. Aids was upon them and new forms of puritanism swirled into every conduit, like acrid disinfectant thrown along the gutters. The premature (and nasty) death of the beautiful, misused and helplessly

3

promiscuous young woman in *Sugar Bush* appeared to have a more general message. It could also be represented as a dramatically heightened paradigm of the plight of women subjected to the ruthless economic power and blatant sexual politics of that latest and oldest ruling class, men.

Fierce young women with cropped heads approvingly used the book as a peg upon which to hang the tormentors. Nervous young men, half-afraid to have an erection, held it up as a mirror for all that was worst in themselves. An old man out of a forgotten past had stepped out of the mists of neglect to reveal such an alert and subtle sympathy for what they knew to be their own dilemmas that they were eager to give homage. The praise of the young swelled the chorus.

Jessica, however, was beside herself with rage.

She had believed that the book her elderly uncle was working on would, in the event of it ever being finished, lead to the trauma of rejection, or, failing that, public humiliation. At first, she had been amiably dismissive when he had mooted the project, seeing it as a late and ludicrous fantasy of his testosterone imperialism. But then, as she thought about his suggestion, she began to play a vengeful game with him. She fed him material woven out of her own career. She wrote long letters to him full of detail about the people, the places, the assumptions of the business, editing out her own cries.

When he was dilatory or discouraged, she took it upon herself to restore his sense of purpose, boosting his greedy gut with expensive lunches and good wines. Flattery, cunning, flirtation and generosity kept him up to the mark. Jessica badly wanted him to last out so that the experiences of her own life could be used to exact a punishment that seemed to come out of *his* own life.

And now she had to start all over again, dismantling his narrative, reclaiming herself.

In the three months since *Sugar Bush* had been published, she had read it so many times, and in such an angry fervour, that she knew it word for word. Whole passages had in any case been taken verbatim from her letters. Much of the rest played

4

back to her her own conversations with him. But mixed in with this, adding the peculiar flavours and mistaken resonances, were his own fugitive literary skills, unacknowledged guilts, and quirkily allusive sexual anxieties. Accident, reputation, temporary fashion had done the rest. The damnable book was lauded on all sides. Everyone said it was a favourite for the Booker Prize, and the only one of the usual dim assortment of judges who really had Kingsley's measure ladled out his final dish of good luck by getting a piece of *saignant* sirloin lodged in her windpipe when there was no one around to help.

In the book, the young model, who was known as Blackeyes, had died with her lungs full of water. Jessica knew that the scene had its origins in one of Kingsley's dreams, because he had told her so, many years ago and long before *Sugar Bush* was contemplated.

This, then, was the way to get back into his head, and destroy whatever was left there.

'And every morning that he struggled awake in the unclean tangle of his bed – '

Kingsley's admonitory old dream, it seemed, took place between snores, farts and lip-smacks in a shabbily cavernous loft high above Great Titchfield Street which night after night turned itself into a brightly illuminated Kensington Gardens. He was transported from his sagging mattress to a deckchair on the grass beyond the Round Pond, within earshot of the thinly silver chimes that came from Kensington Palace, where a princess had fallen deeply asleep.

Toy sailing boats bobbed on the water, paper kites dipped and flew in the cloudless sky, happy dogs scampered after thrown sticks, and an old woman with a black hat was feeding cake crumbs to the insolent city birds. There was nothing, so far, to point up the distress or the anxiety which Jessica was determined to find in the old man's slumbering visions.

'Why here?' she said to herself, no longer speaking aloud, and taking her eyes from the tilted mirror to the frustrating and accusing emptiness of the single white sheet that awaited the first stain of her hatred.

Jessica could not maintain the pain of her concentration. She poured herself a large vodka instead. If she had continued to look at the reflection of her own mouth, and if her mouth had continued to recite the words she had not yet written, Jessica Kingsley could perhaps have seen the beautiful young woman of Maurice James Kingsley's wistful imaginings. She was walking across the grass towards the candy-striped deckchair in which he dozed.

But no. The now unattended little boats continued to send out flashes of white on the gently rippling water, the neglected kites still dipped and tumbled in the endless blue, and the unobserved dogs chased tongue and tail after more or less the same sticks and stones. Unaware that Jessica had withdrawn or lost attention, the old woman in the black hat still had half a brick-hard macaroon and most of a collapsed sponge-cake to remove from the brown paper bag she was holding against her pendulous bosom.

Besotted by detail, which proliferates when no one is looking and spreads on the air quicker than summer insects, Maurice James Kingsley allowed his eyelids to gather weight, and droop. He was seventy-seven years old, after all, and already tired of the ceaseless murmurings.

She came across the tufty grass towards him, the girl he knew as Blackeyes. Oh, what a peach! Her long, shining black hair was swaying softly upon her lustrous shoulders, as though in time to an otherwise unheard balalaika. A froth of flamingo pink lace rode upon her slender young limbs, for she was dressed only in the flimsiest underwear, except for highly polished boots that came half-way up to her knees.

Since this was a dream, no one in the park took the slightest interest in the scantily clad young woman, even though she was an erotic dream girl straight off the posters, whose sculpted lips, jewelled eyes, and glowing flesh were all used to sell various powders and lotions, places and appliances.

Kingsley stared, opened his pale eyes, and felt his nerves jump.

Blackeyes was now only a few paces away, the sharp heels of

her boots leaving marks on the soft ground. She was near enough for him to see the fine down on her forearms, and to smell the faint traces of almond and avocado on the sheen of her skin. Her navel was looking straight at him, and he thought that it could be an eye about to give a knowing wink. Way off, somewhere in the tremble of the trees, a child had opened the lid of a music box, and it was playing 'Clementine', but too slowly.

O My Darling, O My Darling, O My Darling Clementine.

'Oh, I see,' he said to her, ignoring the distant tinkle and the sadness of her expression as a sting of pleasure replaced his initial astonishment. 'You've decided to come, have you, my little chickadee?'

'No. I have decided to go,' she said, as toneless as a depressive.

'Go? Go? What do you mean go?'

The girl stood in front of him, and slowly extended her arms. By God, he rejoiced, his teeth stretching, by Holy Christ, she's a peach, a corker, a cracker, all that stuff. And it's been a long, long time to have been so dry of juices, so limp at the loins, so . . .

'Look at my hands,' she said, her voice still uninflected. 'Look at my fingers.'

The tips of her long fingers were raw and bloodied, the nails badly torn and broken. He wondered whether she had been clawing against a stone wall or an iron door, trying to get out.

'That's all very well,' he pouted, sensing an approaching disappointment. 'I can't do very much about that, now can I, little pussy cat?'

'Look at my hands, sir. Look at my fingers.'

'I can't help it, can I? We don't have to waste time examining your fingers, surely? I've got a far better suggestion. It won't hurt you one little bit.'

'Look at my hands, please. Look at my fingers, sir.'

'A little rogering is more what I had in mind,' he said, trying to pull himself up from the festive deckchair. 'Get some fresh air and sunshine on my poor old bottie, eh? That would be very-very – '

7

The 'nice' could not get out between the sudden clench of his yellowed teeth. The lascivious smile became a rictus of effort. Something was pressing hard down on the bone of his chest.

'I can't seem to get up,' he managed to say, trying to contain his alarm with a semblance of self-derision. 'This poor old carcass of mine is not going to play the game.'

Perfect but for her wounded fingers, the girl of more than his dream looked down at the straining old man with the kind of melancholy passivity which was always to make her even more desirable.

'I can't find Jessica,' she said, before turning away with a swing of her hips.

The movement made him sick with a lust which was stronger by far than anything he had felt for years and years. He pressed his hands down on the wooden supports of the chair, but the merrily striped belly of canvas held him fast.

'Come back!' he called after her. 'Come here, you sweet little bitch! I want you!'

But she continued to walk away from him, and did not turn her lovely head. The lilt of her almost naked body did not fit the sadness that had been in her face. Nobody else around the summery pond paid any heed to her, even when her swaying stride carried her straight into the water. Why was he the only one shouting and gesticulating? Why was the blue draining out of the sky?

'The water came over her shining boots, swallowed up her knees and long thighs, and then made a line around the naked swell of her belly. In next to no time, there was nothing but her head to be seen, then a few thick strands of floating black hair, and soon she was completely submerged, with no sign of fuss or struggle. Whatever traces she may have left on the lives of others, this girl, she had gone now, without a ripple. The water smoothed itself flat, and reflected back the sky.'

Sugar Bush had ended in this way. These were the words Jessica had to make a start with, if she were to prevent a not especially hideous nightmare from leaking so much more nastily into the light of day.

2

The scraggy old bag of bones reared up out of the tumble of bedclothes as the old-fashioned alarm clock jumped and jangled on the bare boards of the floor. Even as the waters enclosed the sad and beautiful lady of his dreams, Kingsley's brown-speckled branch of a hand was clawing out from under the worn eiderdown to grapple with the intruding clangour.

Still sufficiently held within the tendrils of his receding dream to let out a garbled cry of warning, Kingsley nevertheless managed to silence the bell. More awake, he continued to grope with his noduled skein of a hand on the floorboards beside his bed. He was searching for his packet of Gauloises, for it was only when he had sucked down a long draught of smoke into his lungs that he could acknowledge that his day had begun.

The bed was a peninsula in an enormous, almost Manhattan-style loft above commercial rooms and studios in the middle of London's garment district. Old plaster on the walls had scabrously flaked to expose cartographical patches or continents of orange beneath the last layers of disguise, which were approximately the colour of elephant hide.

Threadbare black blinds with dangling ivory hoops were pulled down at the three tall windows fronting the street, reducing the light to a dusky soup. There were no pictures, no cushions, no carpets in the room, but lots of wooden shelves stacked full of books, folders, papers, runs of literary magazines from before and since *Horizon*, and the occasional unemptied ashtray. A big round table, a new swivelling chair, and a bench more suitable for a garden completed the arrangement. It was a place capable of intimidating the nervous or provoking the contempt of the fastidious. Jessica had said nothing derogatory on her last visit here, but she had brought an armful of flowers and a smile that looked like a hurt by the time it reached her eyes.

Kingsley had long since ceased to bother about his habitation. The foxes had their holes, the birds of the air their nests, and he had this, which was one up on the nuisance he called the anaemic Nazarene. His eyes followed a column of cigarette smoke into the surrounding murk as he emptied the last of the dream out of his head, and although they then darted about the room with what seemed to be a critical survey he did not actually see its deficiencies. He was wondering why he had set the alarm, for he considered ten o'clock in the morning to be as bad as the crack of dawn. There must be a reason, therefore, for such self-discipline, but try as he might he could not remember what it was. His gaze settled on the four remaining copies of *Sugar Bush* on the round table, and a renewed inhalation of delight joined the smoke in his lungs.

In good spirit now, Kingsley scratched briefly at his scalp and then at his armpits, rattled out a cough, pulled down some more French tobacco, and settled himself for the opening of what he always referred to as his 'magic casement': the speaking aloud of renowned verse.

He knew many poems and segments of poems by heart, and his otherwise faltering memory had let go of none of them. A booming recitation of any one of these of a morning he regarded as better than brushing the teeth or drenching oneself in soapy hot water. The declining literacy of the generations who were not his contemporaries (that is, the great majority of the population, and everyone in the universities) was a subject of scandal and concern to him, and he frequently tried to tell people so, especially when they were not prepared to listen.

'"Fair seed-time had my soul, and I grew up,"' he began to declaim, his hand insisting on the beat, '"Foster'd alike by beauty and by fear."' If it was Wednesday, this must be Wordsworth.

He pulled hard on his cigarette again, swallowing down too much smoke to continue the recitation. The fact that his alarm clock had been set came back to puzzle him. Like many who are much given to bluster, Kingsley was hollowed out with pockets of an old and inexplicable fear, but his was far more dangerous than most of such inner hauntings. He heard among the solitary furnishings, so to speak, low breathings coming after him, and sounds of indistinguishable motion. The panic that was always near the skin threatened to break, and he held himself very still until the peril had passed.

But Maurice James Kingsley possessed a great source of comfort, a soother, which nobody knew about, because he took great care to make sure that nobody ever saw it.

'Where are you?' he asked suddenly, in a gravelly voice. 'Where have you got to, you wanton little trollop? Eh? Eh?'

He cocked his head to listen, and then answered as though someone had spoken.

'And where's *here*? Where's that supposed to be? As if I give a twopenny coitus. Oh. Yes. You've got your greedy little face up against my poor old crotch again, haven't you, my little chicka dee? Under the bloody clothes again, I presume, madam.'

He rooted about in the dingy tangle of his bedding, dropping cigarette ash on the eiderdown, and pulled up by one fat little brown arm a battered teddy bear. The teddy – which ought to be termed an edwina, in a nod to the conventions of gender – was missing one brown button of an eye, and had lost some of its tightly woven fur.

Kingsley plumped the careworn teddy down into a sitting position on the sag of the far pillow. The single brown eye stared soberly back at him. He looked at it, and his face softened.

'You sweet little bitch,' he said, and patted the creature on the slope of its nose, then swung his spindly legs on to the bare boards of the floor.

'Oh, look at my nails, for God in heaven's sake,' he growled examining the long claws stuck out on the ends of his toes. 'Cast your beady brown eye upon my poor old feet. Who would kiss these little piggy-wiggies, eh, my beloved? Still. There it is, there it is. Long nails probably help one to balance oneself properly, what say you?'

Kingsley stubbed out his cigarette, and rose at last from his bed with an enormous yawn. He slept in his baggy off-white pants and quarter-sleeved, buttoned vest, and did not have to don or adjust any clothing in order to show himself at his windows. His toe-nails rasped on the boards as he padded across the room, where he made the blinds fly up with such force that their dangling ivory rings rapped against the glass of the upper frames.

A bright light of mid-morning flooded into the loft, unaffected by the smears, blotches and newspaper-walloped insects on the window panes. Kingsley had to crinkle his eyes against the unexpected dazzle, but he was feeling a sudden elation of spirit. The sunshine was a reminder of the fame that he considered had newly shone upon him after the years of neglect and near oblivion. Autumn sunshine, he had once observed in one of the more melancholy of his Occasional Pieces, shows the motes in the air and carries the promise of death in its smile. But today the street below, always so active in working hours and empty the rest of the time, eddied and sparkled with a holiday spirit. The people down there looked as though they might be on their way to the fair, with coloured ribbons in their pockets if not in their hair.

The September sun, bright and low, made a precise line of almost blue shadow on the opposite pavement. Kingsley put his forehead against the glass, so that the glitter might enter his head: or was it, he wondered, that the glory in his head had put all this luminosity into the ordinary day? Tumbles and glances and glints of light, quicker than thoughts. Beams of praise.

'"Sweet day, so cool, so calm, so bright,"' he exclaimed, '"The bridall of the earth and sky: The dew shall weep thy fall tonight – ."'

The old man was using what his few acquaintances had learnt to recognize with misery as his Literary Voice. There had also been times late of an evening when distraught strangers had yelled *Shut up!* across the entire length of a saloon bar when subjected to it. Declamatory, nasal, swooping and trembling, and above all trumpetingly loud, Kingsley's Literary Voice suggested antique spellings and tadpole-sized commas even when there were none.

But on the fourth line of the window-pane poem Kingsley's voice dried.

He peered down into the street with a new, less indulgent expression. His head lifted away from the pane and then bumped back against it once more, hard enough to make the glass shudder, and shimmer with a disturbed light. A young woman who fitted the bright morning was walking along the shadowed pavement opposite his window: and Kingsley, staring, began to think that she was the same dark lady as his dream, his text.

'Blackeyes!' he hissed, half in wonder, half in fear.

The better to follow her, he crabbed sideways to each of the adjoining windows. Little hollow thuds in the hairy caves of his ears warned him that his pulse was quickening. But, but, but, it went. *But* if the slender, long-legged lady tip-tapping her high heels on the hard slabs down there was out of his own story, then how could she be embodied *out there* . . .?

She was moving so fast that there was no time to work this out. His tobacco-laden breath was making faint whistling noises in the narrowed passage of his throat, so that it was difficult to think properly. But the half-idea flew up, like a bird on the sill, that something or someone was interfering with *Sugar Bush*, or with the private property of his own dreams. The girl down there was receding from his view, as though she were going out of copyright.

Kingsley did not consider whether the distance, the dazzle in his elderly eyes, the drench of shadow in which she moved, and the speed of her swaying walk, had together affected his perceptions.

'That's *her*,' he said, although she was no longer in view.

After a while, the drumming still in his head, he went across to the round table and picked up one of the mint-fresh copies of his book. The smooth shine of the jacket was cool and reassuring on his fingers. Black print on clean white pages with decent margins waited inside the covers.

'The young woman who had passed along the pavement, below windows made blank by the morning sunshine, was possessed by the kind of beauty which provokes as much hatred as admiration. Too many men wanted to feast upon her,' he read on one of the early pages. 'Those in the street were unable to stop themselves from staring at her as she went by, although some had the grace to be merely wistful . . .'

Kingsley read on, and his alarm subsided. The ordered sentences flowed back into him, and carried his thoughts along. Blackeyes glistened before him once more, the light playing on her skin, and darkening her eyes. Why had he killed her?

The book in his hand, but his eyes no longer on the page, Kingsley stood still, moistening his lips. An old yearning whispered its way towards him. '"She walks in beauty like the . . ."' he said, but not in his literary voice, nor out loud at all. He sighed, but not a theatrical sigh, and put the book back on top of the small pile. His shoulders had drooped.

'Why the hell can't *you* look like that!' he shouted, suddenly, glaring across the brightened room to his rumpled bed. 'You're nothing but a worn out, one-eyed, misbegotten lump of – '

The abuse was not continued. He rushed across the loft, plucked up the teddy bear from the pillow, and hugged it tightly to his breast, rocking a little.

'Oh I'm sorry I'm sorry I'm sorry,' he gabbled. 'I don't mean it, petal. How could I mean it? You're all I've got, all I – there! there! there!'

Kingsley sat down heavily on the bed, cradling and stroking the little beast as the springs sang at his haunches. Soon, though, he fell silent. He was beginning to fret again about the fact that he had set the alarm clock. Was he expecting someone? Perhaps he had better empty his bladder, enduring the stinging and burning sensations. And then, yes, get dressed. A wise man would be ready for the expected unexpected, including the snap of handcuffs at the wrist.

3

The police were pegging off a section of the park, wide around the pond. A body lay covered on the grass. The sky was no longer a paintbox blue, and there were no illustrated dogs chasing sticks, no old men slumbering in candy-striped chairs. Trees had shed their leaves, and the remains of an early morning frost spangled the grass. It was too grey, too chilled, too inactive to be anyone's dream.

A middle-aged man with a stale pudding of a face but glints of intelligence in his eyes was stooping to lift a corner of the covering over the body.

'Let this be a lesson to you, old son,' he said, with no hint of amusement to the uniformed constable standing leaden-footed and cold-nosed at his side. 'Don't mess around with toy boats on the bleed'n pond.'

'No, sir,' said the constable, trying not to sniff.

Detective Inspector Blake looked at the face of the dead woman. He raised the cover still more, revealing young and naked limbs. His mouth pulled itself in against his teeth.

'She was something special, whoever or whatever she was. By Christ, this was a beauty, eh?'

'Yes, sir.'

Blake (who was eternally grateful to his parents for resisting the temptation to give him Sexton as a first name) was irritated by these mechanical responses. He felt the morning chill as much as anyone else rooting about in the grass, but that was no reason to show a lack of keenness.

'Buck yourself up, lad.'

'Sorry, sir.'

'The question is – Christ, wipe your snitch, will you? – the question is, did she wait until dark and do this to herself? Or did somebody else give her a bit of a helping hand?'

The younger policeman looked around and about with a show of interest.

'Where are her clothes, then?' he asked.

Twenty minutes later they found a quilted dressing gown rolled up like a sleeping animal under the trees, with nothing in the pockets except a paperclip.

4

Kingsley's narrative had said that Blackeyes gained her first solo job as a model on one of those September mornings 'when the buildings and the sky seemed to be made of the same material, a compound of smoke and uncoloured, man-made fibre'. Reading this, with a curl of the lip against the style of prose, Jessica had to acknowledge that he had filled in her account of her own first dry-run audition, at an advertising agency off New Cavendish Street, with a kind of gleeful contempt she had not been able to express herself. Give the old bugger his due.

The room and the people were as she had described them, but he had diminished her into an entranced automaton. The trouble was that the strange and lost blankness he had cast over Blackeyes was beginning to fall upon *her*, too. Jessica was finding it more and more difficult to piece together an alternative account: but this, being the later one, was what was needed to rescue the sad girl in the fiction and the angry woman in her real life. The last word was the one which mattered.

She tried to think what it must have been like in the audition room before any of the models made their separate entries. The usual feeling of death in the air which the season brings might also have been noticed by the men who gathered there, but she rather doubted it.

Mostly middle aged and well paunched, they sat in tubular steel and canvas chairs in a room of an equally brutal design on the top floor of the building. They were at right angles to each other on two sides of the white upon white walls, facing inwards to a long, low table which had a mirrored top and chunky glass legs. It was placed, deliberately, not quite at the centre of the room.

The spotlights angled down from the walls were all trained

17

upon the table, making its reflecting top glitter like a clear pool in the Mediterranean sun. Here, the only man not in a business suit was carefully, perhaps even satirically, dusting down the table with a chamois leather.

'Dust, gentlemen. If you will forgive such an old-fashioned word,' he said, with a flick. 'Perhaps I should call it tiny particles of unbiodegradable matter. Why does it get everywhere?'

He stopped what he was doing and looked at the seated men with a twinkle of pleased malice, as one who knows that the question is both profound and unanswerable. What, he seemed to be saying, is the fatal defect in this, our universe? The mist pressing still at the metal-framed windows suited the workings of Andrew Stilk's mind, and the solemn faces in front of him were a severe temptation.

Stilk moved across to a smaller side table, glancing sideways at his audience with a mocking lift of the brow. A barely suppressed *voilà!*, and he removed a dust-cover from the object on the table. It was a bottle.

'And here we are, gentlemen,' he said. '*Your* bottle as redesigned by what this agency is pleased to call its think-tank. And adjusted a teeny-weeny bit more by yours truly.'

The businessmen did not know whether they were supposed to be amused or impressed, and one of them compromised by scraping his chair on the polished, wood-block floor. It made a suitably ambivalent sound.

'There is as yet no label, since there is as yet no name,' Stilk said, placing the bottle very precisely off-centre on the mirrored table-top. Tall and tapering, except for a slight bulge near the middle, the bottle was filled with an amber liquid. There was a glitter of small, shining octagonals around the neck, and these set up a series of endless reflections with the mirror below. 'And the name, as you well know, is almost as important as what is being named.'

Stilk brushed the bottle with the tips of his fingers. His own modest proposal, he said, was Lagoon or, possibly, Laguna. This seemed to him to merit applause, and he waited for it.

18

'This bottle will, after all, hold *your* product, gentlemen,' he said, when none came. 'I think it would positively *glow* for a few distinct murmurs of approbation.'

The businessmen continued to stare, in awkward silence, at the bottle, which was gleaming in the puddle of its own reflection. They were troubled by Stilk: his language, his manner, his guessed-at sexual predilections. Somewhere near, the men knew, beautiful young women were changing into bikinis and high-heeled shoes, ready to perform. Why all this talk?

'Mr Stilk,' said Mr Jamieson, in an attitude which revealed him to be their leader. 'Your soliciting of our approval is positively threatening. But you are right. Jolly good. I think it's very well done.'

Jamieson slapped his large hands together, briefly. Instant murmurs of assent came from his colleagues, and the applause lightened everyone's mood. 'They looked at the bottle again, and it glowed like a sacred object, awaiting the sacrificial maidens,' said the text of Kingsley's story, in what most readers took to be irony, but which Jessica knew to be a wet-mouthed excitement of the same order as that felt by 'Jamieson' and his crew. God rot their souls! And stuff their severed cocks in their screaming mouths.

Jessica let the storm pass through her, and then, at its last tremble, dragged her attention back to the page.

'The models were getting themselves ready directly across the corridor in a room of similar proportions. Blackeyes, pushing through the door in a late arrival, saw as she glanced hurriedly around that unlike herself all the other young women were blonde. A dozen or so pairs of blue eyes turned out of an Aryan dream to look at her as she suddenly hesitated on the threshold.'

A much older woman with a baleful forehead broke off talking to one of these half-naked blondes and came over to the uncertain newcomer, brandishing an accusing clipboard.

'And who might you be?' she asked, without friendliness.

Blackeyes wanted to go back out immediately, and without

explanation. But, like Jessica had done in the same circumstances, she made herself stay. 'I knew that if I left, no other door would open, anywhere,' she told her uncle, who was in the middle of a mouthful of veal and did not seem to understand. He had looked far more interested in his food than in the scraps she was offering him.

'Hi!' said Blackeyes, falsely bright. 'I'm Blackeyes.'

'What do you mean, I'm Black Eyes!' The casting director looked down at her clipboard, scarcely bothering to hide a snort of disdain. 'Black eyes who? Black eyes what, for goodness sake?'

'Just Blackeyes. One word. My – it's my professional name.'

'Oh. It's your professional name.'

'Well. It will be. Yes.'

'And who sent you?'

'Sent me?'

Blackeyes was finding it difficult not to wilt. The inexplicable hostility in her questioner's face so blanked out her mind that she could hardly remember the name of the incompetent and over-hopeful model agency which had told her to come. This was worse than being back at school.

'This is just typical. The bane of my life. The call was for blondes, dear. I can't imagine what they think they were doing. You are not even on my list.'

'Well, here I am!' said Blackeyes, determinedly bright, although it was not in her nature to be so.

'Blondes. With very fair skin. Natural blondes. I don't suppose you could change your *professional* name to Blue Eyes, could you?'

As ill at ease as any novice, and unequipped to deal with sarcasm, Blackeyes looked around at the other young women. They stared back at her, but without personal interest, and she turned her enormous, dark eyes back to her questioner. 'Eyes that compelled an almost stupefied attention, eyes that steadily gleamed with mystery and an obscure power suggesting amalgams of pain and pleasure: a Mesmer's eyes from long-ago salons and half-forgotten magics.'

20

(Jessica, each time she reached this point, looked sidelong at the oval mirror on the metal stalk, eyes upon eyes instead of lips. They were green. They were green.)

The casting director began to frown at the dark, unblinking scrutiny. 'Oh, well,' she said, in a different voice. 'If you really want to waste your time, and ours – I hope you've brought a bikini.'

'Of course I have,' said Blackeyes, not shifting her gaze.

'Of course you have! But since they've got everything else wrong, your people, it might have been a spacesuit, mightn't it? With bells on.'

The casting director said this generally, with an outward splay of an unadorned hand, seeking a laugh from the others, but also to escape the thrill of shame which puzzled her. The nearest girls hardly bothered to smile, and one of them winked at Blackeyes instead.

Blackeyes turned her face away, without a covert smile of acknowledgement. She wanted no alliances.

Across the corridor, in the room where the bottle waited, the final blind came down over the last of the windows, and the battery of spotlights on the wall quickly dimmed. For a moment, all was darkness. Andrew Stilk, a remote-control pad in each hand, and taking everything far more seriously than his previous tones had implied, counted a slow one–two–three–four in his head before pressing a button.

A vermilion blaze ignited the glass table. The bottle upon it glowed in the fire. Beyond, the rest of the room shuddered into flowing shadow. The watching businessmen had become dark humps, emanating tension and expectation, their doubly hidden thoughts full of girls.

A chair scraped on the wooden floor again, and Stilk frowned at what he mistook as a lack of due attention. He needed stillness and silence from these people, and would not begin until they gave it to him.

'Style,' he said at last. 'Structure,' he said. 'Improvisation,' he said.

'What I mean is,' he said, 'is improvisation within structure, fluid unexpectedness within style. The product illuminated in the clean dazzle of the spiritually wholesome, the socially enhancing, the life-giving. Mysterious. Mysteriously potent. And yet, and yet – *accessible*.'

He peered across at the darkened humps, which were beginning to take on individual shapes and features. The backwash of light glinted on spectacle frames and bald patches and a watch strap.

'Let me explain,' he said, with an unwise smile.

'Please do, Mr Stilk,' came a voice out of the shadows. It was Jamieson, and there was enough of an edge to put Stilk on his guard.

'The basic idea here,' he said, concentrating on the interrupter, 'is that of a timeless space in a timeless nowhere and everywhere – '

A sigh warned him to come back from the woods where a French semiologist lay mouldering, in piles of fallen leaves that had long since given up their signals. Stilk knew that he was employed to rattle the stick in the swill-bucket, but his self-hatred was not eased by the sure fact that nobody in his audience ever had the slightest idea of the provenance of this particular reference.

'In other words,' he said, in a rising tone, 'this is for any woman in any social class, anywhere.'

The sense of relief in the listeners was almost palpable, like steam coming up from a herd. It irritated Stilk, who felt demeaned.

'But when this structure, or shall we say, this net of *signals*', he began again, putting his weight on his toes to point the emphasis, or the little rebellion, 'within this complexly simple set or situation – '

'Oh, for God's sake, man!'

Jamieson's second, more vigorous interjection provoked a few hurtful titters. Stilk returned his body to its heels. He was not a brave man, and knew authority when he heard it.

'OK, O-kay,' he said, as though everything else had been a

joke. 'Let's get to the bottom line. Let's chew on the nitty-gritty. What we want here is a blonde with terrific tits who's got the sense to make love to the fucking bottle.'

The laughter was loud enough to reach the dozen blondes (and the one raven-head) who did not yet know the order of the privilege which awaited them. They looked at each other in surprise, and some apprehension, for normally there were not so many people present at this kind of audition.

They were by now ready for their call, each in a bikini and stilt-like heels. Only Blackeyes, the latecomer, was still undressing. There was about as much privacy in here as in a football changing room, and she tried to remove her own clothes as though she were alone: one of the tell-tale signs of a novice. The others simply appraised each other with an entirely professional detachment

'You got pretty little boobs, love,' said the girl who had winked at her, as Blackeyes put on the top half of her bikini.

Blackeyes looked quickly away, but then decided it would be better to speak.

'Yes, I know,' she said, like one ready to be offended. 'Too little.'

'Oh, no! Look at these, will you!' the other girl laughed, thrusting out her breasts in a cheerfully matter-of-fact gesture. 'You'd think I'd had a silicone job, wouldn't you? Like bleed'n great melons, ent they? My fellow says they bruise his ears. The cheek.'

Without more encouragement than a faint smile, the bouncy little Londoner introduced herself as Rosie Hughes: 'Geddit? Rosy Hues. You know. Colours.'

Blackeyes did not want to talk, and had no desire to make friends, but she needed some information.

'Listen – '

'Go on,' said Rosie, as she hesitated.

'I sort of sneaked into this. Somebody else who couldn't make it told me and and – I shouldn't be here – ' she stopped, and looked away.

'What's the matter?'

Blackeyes returned her gaze to Rosie, making the cheerful girl's almost permanent grin waver. She wondered if this striking newcomer was on hard drugs: the eyes were glittering far back in their depths, a characteristic which a fashion writer was later to describe as 'like moonlight on dark waters'.

'I'd like to know what it is we are auditioning for – ?'

Rosie was as puzzled by the question as by the strange intensity with which it was asked.

'Dirty old geezers, I expect,' she said, with an automatic laugh.

What product, what job, was what Blackeyes meant, but before she could explain the extent of her ignorance, the casting director was clapping her hands for attention.

'Girls! All right, girls! Listen to me, if you please!' she was saying, in what could have been an imitation of the headmistress of a girls' school. 'Now, the first thing – listen, please! – the first thing, it's one of these lighting questions, I'm afraid. I've been asked to make quite sure that none of you is using any of the glitter dusting powders – '

The few mostly satiric groans of protest gave Rosie the chance to push away the faint chill that had descended upon her.

'Bang goes me sparky cleavage!' she called, to general laughter.

'No glitter,' the headmistress smiled an allowed smile. 'Now, then. You will go in one at a time, naturally, and you will each be given four minutes. They'll tell you what they want . . .'

She held up her hand at a few murmurs of disappointment, and, looking across at Blackeyes, said that four minutes was long enough, 'and some of you won't even need that.'

The first call was for a model called Veronica, who appeared to be a favourite of the casting director. A tall and graceful blonde, behaving as though she were not too young to have seen Grace Kelly in her prime, she held up crossed fingers in a democratic style, soliciting a few scarcely genuine mumbles of Good Luck as she went out of the room.

'Toffee-nosed cow,' said Rosie, amiably enough. 'Can't blame her, though. If I was her, I'd pack it in like a shot.'

24

Blackeyes made a polite noise, but she was only half-listening. Her attention was fixed on the departing Veronica, in something of the same way that a cat might watch a bird in a cage.

'Her dad's as rich as creases. He invented fish fingers or something – it's the national bloody diet, ennit? She don't need this. It don't matter to her if she gets it or not.'

'I need it,' said Blackeyes suddenly, properly listening now. 'It matters to me.'

The way she said it made Rosie stop smiling.

'Attagirl,' Rosie said, her own eyes hardening.

5

Sliding out in a dull metallic trundle, like the drawer of an enormous filing cabinet, the now refrigerated and alabaster white body of the beautiful young woman came out of Jessica's sleeping darkness and fully into Detective Inspector Blake's view. A tag was tied to one of the big toes, giving that most clownish of joints an additionally comic guise.

Even in these anaphrodisiac conditions, stripped of life and a designer's pretence, it was possible to see how such limbs could have been misused in erotic poses and salesmen's gigantic posters. The tag on the toe provided the major difficulty.

'What do you mean, a note?' Blake was asking in irritated incredulity. 'How the fuck can you have found a note on her when she was stark bloody bare and naked?'

His face changed as possible ways came to him. The man in the white coat on the other side of the corpse gave a series of little nods.

'We've all got hiding places we can call our own,' the pathologist said.

Blake sniffed an Oh or a Yes, and then swore in distaste as the other held up a tiny plastic pouch with the air of a conjuror.

'You would need to fold it up very small, and this was folded up very small. You also need it be be non-absorbent – '

'Not half,' Blake sniffed again.

' – and this is waterproof.'

They looked at each other. Blake showed no eagerness to take the little pouch.

'What are we playing here?' he asked. 'What's My Bloody Line, or Animal Vegetable and Mineral?'

'We're playing Hunt the Slipper.'

'All right. All right. Where was it? Front or back passage?'

'Front, Inspector.'

Blake took half a step backwards, as though he had been personally affronted. His eyes flickered briefly over the stretched-out corpse, in accusation, and then he accepted the proffered pouch.

'And this was in her – in her wasname – ?'

'Her vagina. Yes.'

Blake pursed his lips in a faint suck of sound, and suddenly scratched the back of his neck. He kept his eyes away from the living one, and the dead.

'What's it say?' he asked, eventually.

'You could say it was a message, I suppose. And you could also deduce why she put it where she put it. The writing is very very tiny. Very meticulous.'

'Lord's Prayer on the back of a postage stamp.'

'What?'

'Sort of thing,' said Blake.

They looked at each other again. This time, it was the pathologist who turned away, made uncomfortable by the policeman's banked-down rage.

'It's a list of names,' he said.

'Men?'

'Men.'

Men. Of course it was men. They both looked at the body of the young woman in acknowledgement, even apology.

'But what about her hands? The nails and that?' Blake asked.

'Market gardening.'

'What do you mean?'

'Back-yard dirt. London dirt.'

Blake squinted sidelong at the cold white limbs, momentarily imagining them in sexual movement.

'Well,' he said, casting out the picture, 'there's plenty of that about.'

The limbs would not stop moving. The hips swivelled and the little round belly shuddered. The legs widened and tried to grip, and then all of her groaned inside and sat up. A quartz clock began its insectoid click-click-click, measuring the night.

'Look at my hands,' she said. 'Look at my fingers.'

6

'Hello,' said Andrew Stilk, unctuous and yet threatening. 'Nice to see you. How are you? Glad you could come, darling. My name is Andrew Stilk. These gentlemen are from Featherwheel, and they are very interested in what you might be able to do for them. We would like you to tell us who you are. Your name, please.'

He gradually lost his smile while he was speaking.

It was Blackeyes who had come into the room, the last one to be auditioned. Stilk's face had changed because he could see that she was stiff with nerves, or there was something more seriously wrong. Her big, still, dark eyes had settled, to stare at his mouth.

'What's wrong, angel? Cat got your tongue?'

In the shadowy light beyond the glare, Jamieson was leaning forward in his chair, fascinated. The thrust of his head caught the outer edges of the vermilion dazzle, and his heavily framed glasses flashed as though from within.

Blackeyes let her gaze wander off and then fall again on Stilk.

'My name is Blackeyes,' she said, and the lack of inflection matched the unfathomable darkness of her eyes.

'Oh, is it now?' Stilk was not prepared to be kindly. 'And were you told by any chance that I wanted to look at *fair* damsels, only *fair* damsels?'

She shook her head, keeping the same glazed expression.

'Ladies with blonde locks. Ladies with blue eyes. Ladies with complexions of peaches and yoghurt.'

'What sort of yoghurt?' she asked.

A few suppressed sniggers from the darker side of the room made Stilk feel a little foolish, though he knew that it should be the girl who received the derision. He glared at her, with a growing hostility.

'What do you mean?' he jeered.

'Nobody said anything to me about yoghurt,' she said, still unflustered. 'I would have remembered.'

Stilk could not be completely sure whether this girl was utterly stupid or cunningly bright in some way that he could not work out. He had been wrong-footed, as the renewed sniggers confirmed.

'Dear, dear, dear, isn't that too, too tedious,' he said, showing her his teeth. 'Tedious for you. Tedious for me. I'm afraid you've rather wasted your time. I'm *so* sorry but there's no point in your – '

'Mr Stilk,' said Jamieson, suddenly.

Stilk had his back to the chairs, facing the infuriating girl, so the businessman could not see the manner in which his eyes hooded, nor did he hear the faint, put-upon sigh on his lips.

'There was something – ?' he asked, politely enough, half on the turn.

Jamieson smiled affably and spread his large hands in token regard for the interruption. He pointed out that they might as well 'have a look' at her, since they had not yet found the ideal candidate, and Miss, um, Blackeyes was the last one for the day. There was nothing to be lost by letting her 'have a go'.

Straightening the denimed slopes of his shoulders, Stilk seemed about to argue, but then compromised with a would-be superior leer.

'I think we need a lot of patience here, Mr Jamieson,' he said. 'But yes, why not, why not?'

Blackeyes said a thank-you, but she looked across the room to where the residues of light burnished Jamieson's spectacles, correctly identifying their owner as the man who was really in charge, the man to please. Nothing could have more irritated Stilk, except Jamieson's gesture of response: another spread of the hands, but a self-conscious one, cloaking a sexual attraction with the guise of avuncular urbanity.

'You cunning little bitch,' he thought.

'Blackeyes,' he said, at the same time. 'What we have here, sweetie, is a dry-run audition. Do you understand? Now, no sort of formal structure is going to be imposed on you, OK? In other words, there is no carapace, no hard shell – right? Or hard sell, come to that. All is fluid. It is about *your* inventiveness, *your* perceptual parameters, *your* – '

'Yes,' she said.

'What – ?'

'Yes,' she said. 'I said yes.'

'Yes. You said yes,' he rolled up his eyes. 'Yes, what? Yes, what about?'

Blackeyes looked back at him, unwavering. She appeared to consider the matter.

'About all that,' she said.

Several of the watching businessmen had to make more of an effort to swallow their laughter, and Stilk again felt that it was mockery at his expense. He glared at her, but she remained disconcertingly expressionless.

'Try not to interrupt. Please.'

He paused, expecting her to say a sorry, but she did not speak, and still did not move her eyes.

'Now. Let's begin again,' he said, defeated. 'In terms of the basic order of things, the reality. Now, there is a bottle on the table, and – '

'Yes,' she said.

Stilk pushed his hand into his hair, in theatrical exasperation. The extremity of it was only partly a pretence.

'There – is – a – bottle – on the table,' he said, enunciating each word in a way that dared her to interrupt. 'There is light, which can and will change colour and intensity. There will be music. And – ta-ra! ta-ra! – there is *you*.'

'Me. Yes.'

'My sweet Christ, yes!' he almost shouted, but then pulled back into control, and actually smiled at her. 'We want, I want, to see what happens when the bottle, the you, and the music are put to-geth-er. You can do exactly what you yourself choose to do. You can do anything you like, so long as it relates to – *is something the matter?*'

Blackeyes, instead of fixing her gaze so steadily upon his

30

mouth, was now peering around and about with such a new air of distraction that he realized she was not listening to a word he said.

'What?' she asked, still looking away.

'Really, my sweet! Are you still with us, or aren't you?'

She turned her dark stare back to him, and said yes. Yes, she was here.

'The tale was later told that Andrew Stilk went berserk in front of the eighteen-year-old, half-naked model,' the old man's novel said, in the distant, characteristically discursive tones of the style he shared with many of his generation. 'According to Jamieson, whose conversation was regularly embellished with an uncharitable excess which would have been even more damaging had he the wit simply to be accurate, the poor fellow literally tore his hair.'

In fact, he did not touch his hair. What he did was to beat a clenched fist at the end of a stiff arm very hard against the front of his thigh.

'Yes! No! What? Yes! No!' he smacked himself. 'What is it? What is the matter? What the fuck is wrong with you — !'

'Mr Stilk,' said Jamieson, half-rising, as though he were about to restrain the hysteric with his large hands. But he sat down again as Blackeyes answered. She spoke with an almost idiotic calm.

'I'm sorry, but I can't see the — I can't see it. Where is the camera? I'd like to be able to see it.'

Whether because of the childish innocence of her tone, or as a result of Jamieson's rebuke, Stilk regained his self-possession, and with it, his wary pretension.

'I am the camera,' he said, lifting his clenched hand to his chest.

'Oh,' she said.

'These gentlemen — they are the camera.' He tapped his forehead. '*This* is the lens and the shutter. Is that all right? Do you approve?'

Blackeyes looked at him as though he were a puzzling obstruction in the way of some longer and mysterious view that

31

was hers alone. A strange, lost, near-blankness was upon her, one which belonged to witches and she-devils in their moments of contemplation. It was so marked that Stilk felt a bump of tension in his chest.

She gave a little shrug of her naked shoulders, in what appeared to be a formidable indifference.

'OK,' she said. 'If you say so.'

Within a few minutes, after he had gritted out a list of simple demands, schmaltzy music syruped from a compact disc player, controlled by a pad. It was an over-orchestrated version of 'By a Sleepy Lagoon', trilling with what were labelled as 'silver strings'.

'In your own time, and in your own way,' Stilk repeated, telling her to begin.

Blackeyes remained totally still in her flimsy bikini and stiletto heels, staring at the bottle on the mirror-topped table. 'The thought occurred to many of those watching her,' Kingsley had written, 'that she was an enchanted creature in a fairy-tale. Her skin was as white as snow, her hair as black as ebony, and her lips as red as the blood that had not yet been spilt.'

(Objecting in advance to such a description, Jessica had joshed him by pointing out that 'there is no fucking' in fairy-tales.

'Ah, no,' he had said, 'but there is a lot of cruelty.')

Jamieson, too, was equally still, but in another story. His colleagues, ranged alongside him in the tubular steel chairs, were divided betwen those who had eyes only for the lustrous girl and those who had noticed his lascivious fervour. The evocative music, too, added to the growing sexual tension by haplessly suggesting the *triste* on the far side of many an imagined copulation.

Blackeyes still did not move, letting them dream their dreams.

'Did you not eat your cornflakes this morning?' Stilk asked, by now genuinely wishing her ill.

She kept her eyes on the glowing bottle, and did not blink. Her skin did not rise and fall. It seemed that she must be holding her breath.

32

Stilk buttoned out the music, holding the remote-control pad well away from his body. His elbow jutted out at a bizarre angle, as though it alone could accurately signal the pain and the affront he was enduring.

'Are you not well?' he asked between closed teeth. 'Or are you waiting for the next bus?'

She took her gaze away from the bottle, but gave the impression that she was looking at everything in between with an equal and studious attention before finally letting it settle on Stilk.

'What happened to the music?' she asked.

Stilk sent up an elongated dialogue-balloon of noise. The skin over his cheekbones stretched tighter, went whiter.

'It's just – I was just asking about the music,' she said, bewildered by his wanton shriek.

Stilk pulled the disjointed elbow back against his lizard-skin belt, to help hold in the quiver which was humiliating the rest of his body.

'I don't know who you think you are, or what you think you are doing,' he began, then chewed some air, and pulled himself back at the brink of whatever abuse he intended.

'Blackeyes,' he said, instead. 'Listen. Listen to me –'

'Yes.'

He swallowed more air, and jabbed at one of the buttons on his pad. The sleepy lagoon poured back into the room. A saxophone flowed in, silkily narcotic amongst the nervy strings.

'Extemporize!' Stilk shouted.

But once again, to everyone's discomfort, it appeared that Blackeyes was going to do nothing except sink further down into her mute trance. And then, at last, just as Stilk opened his mouth, her high heels began to click on the glossy wood blocks of the flooring.

She incorporated the languorous sway of the music into her movement, her eyes always on the bottle. They were the eyes of a predator, and then they were the eyes of the prey. She stopped. She swayed. She started again.

The watching businessmen were fascinated. The click of her

heels beneath the firm, long legs, the slow sashay of her mostly naked body, and the still dream-like passivity of her expression, were working with the sickly sweetness of the orchestration to make fantasies half-promise, half-threaten to come true for her middle-aged audience. You can have me, slowly tapped her heels. You can have me, lazily swung her hips. You can have me. You can have me.

She completed a full circling of the glass table. The light was like a polish on her young skin. The music saturated her. She was already a figure on a coloured poster.

Everyone waited.

'Everyone is waiting,' said her head, 'everyone is waiting, is waiting. Tell me what to do, to do.' This was Kingsley's account.

'You pigs,' said her mind. 'You pigs. You filthy, rutting pigs.' This was what Jessica knew to have been in her head at the time which was the original occasion for the later fiction.

She stretched out a hand towards the bottle of amber liquid, and put a single long finger on top of it, the scarlet of her nail coming to meet itself in the necklace of small reflecting surfaces.

Touch me like that, urged Jamieson behind the flash of his glasses.

Blackeyes, on the very edge of the comic, began to caress the top of the bottle. Her lips were slightly parted, and she leant forward, showing the full swell of her breasts. She lifted her head, and the movement made her hair sway. Her eyes, catching the glare at a new angle, glittered as she looked across the room into the shadow, too obviously seeking out Jamieson. In almost the same instant, she took her finger away from the bottle and put it to her lips, and began to lick it, and to suck it.

'Mmmm,' she said. 'Mmmmyumm.'

And then she lowered her hand and stared at them all, like an acrobat who has just bounced off the wire, feet together and body poised, waiting for the applause.

Stilk killed the schmaltz coming from the loudspeakers. A vengeful hilarity had already sprung into his face. He broke the puzzled, embarrassed silence, making sure that he kept the delight out of his voice.

34

'May I venture to ask, because I'm sure we'd all like to know – but what, exactly, do you think is in the bottle?'

She narrowed her eyes. The self-induced trance wavered back towards the more human dimensions of anxiety and doubt. It was like watching a doll quiver into life.

'Something delicious?' she said.

Everyone began to laugh: and laughter quickly bellowed out into helplessness. 'Guffaws are as disturbing a noise', claimed Kingsley, 'as the smack of an open hand on another's flesh.'

'And you should know, you old fart,' said Jessica to herself, in a flush of recollected humiliation.

She remembered the animal-like braying, which often grew and grew as it fed upon her nakedness. She remembered, too, that 'Jamieson' had been the first to finish, his neck reddening, and that his silence amongst the laughing faces had been the most ominous feeling of all.

His colleagues continued their roaring until they began to see, in the strong light upon her, the swift glitter of unshed tears in her eyes.

'My dear young lady,' said Stilk, with delighted condescension, 'it is a body lotion. A moisturiser and a sun-filter, which is also an anti-cellulite.'

'You rub it. Rub it in!' Jamieson called, with a jerk of his heavy frame.

The glitter had gone from her eyes. She made no attempt to speak, but shook her head when Stilk jeeringly invited her to drink it if she wanted. He was still so delighted that he failed to notice that the mood had changed in the shadowed areas behind him.

'When I said to rub it in, Mr Stilk, I didn't mean that *you* were to do so,' Jamieson said. 'I rather think the joke is over, don't you?'

Stilk's grin twisted into a new shape, and Blackeyes looked across at Jamieson. For the first time since entering the room, she smiled.

'Do you want me to use it?'

'I'm afraid you've squandered your allocation,' Stilk said, too

35

quickly. 'You were given four minutes, and I don't think we need to see – '

'Yes!' Jamieson shouted. 'Use it!'

'Use it. Use it!' a chorus of voices added, as Stilk turned away in sulky offence.

'Really, I don't know why you want me here at all – !', his voice fluting up a pitch.

Jamieson soothed a now, now and a come, come, as he might have done to a child who had stamped its foot in a paddy.

'No! This is too – !' Stilk responded, in kind, his nostrils pinched with anger.

'Andrew. Andrew. You know very well how much we value your – don't we, gentlemen? This whole set-up is yours. These are *your* ideas, old chap, your um, um, *parameters* – but the young lady might as well continue now that we've had our amusement, might she not?'

The way in which Kingsley's *Sugar Bush* described the slither of Jamieson's eyes to look at the young model, making the light fall across his glasses as his neck followed the import of his already smugly proprietorial glance, was exactly as Jessica had told him. A little drunk at the end of the fourth of their nine lunches (all at her expense), she had matched the slight tilt of the room in the restaurant with a slide of her own mind towards more open expressions of her hatred than she had intended him to hear.

'I could see what the fat bastard was after,' she said.

'And did he get it?' Kingsley had simpered, and the sudden brightness in his pale eyes made her stop. He was practically dribbling over his Roquefort.

In the book, the bloody book, Kingsley had reduced the girl to a zombie yet again, turning her matter-of-fact description and matter-of-fact contempt into a mute psychosis. How many times, she wondered, would allegedly sympathetic accounts of the manifold ways in which women were so regularly humiliated be nothing more than yet further exercises of the same impulse, the identical power?

'Jamieson slid his eyes to look at the young lady, as he had just so threateningly called her, but once more the bright light fell across his glasses as his neck bobbed forward to deliver the possessive leer. She knew what the now hidden expression was, and felt it go through her, to the marrow. Any moment now, the music would begin again, suggesting the sea: a blanched ocean, like a bedsheet, rumpling against the naked sand, the grains already prickling her skin. The sea, the sea, it had to be the sea which was roaring in her ears, and sucking and hissing between the bones of her head. And the water which rushed in was full of slippery fishes with unblinking eyes and open mouths.'

Reading this, but already knowing every word, Jessica sat as neat and as demure as ever in the midst of a litter of torn pages. She did not need to lift her lip in order to sneer at Kingsley's prose. It was the mannered plural of 'fish' that particularly offended her fast developing literary sensibility.

'Slippery fishes,' she repeated, no longer glancing sidelong at the reflection of her own lips.

Codswallop, in fact.

7

Maurice James Kingsley (the three names were printed together far more often than not) could tidy himself up and even wash under his arms when absolutely necessary. His appearance in the taxi he shared with his beautiful niece on the day she first agreed to help him with his 'big project' was not especially a reason for comment, let alone scandal.

He wore a floppy, large-brimmed hat over the spiky grey scrag of his hair, and a floppy, large-winged, polka-dot bow tie at the loose grey scrag of his neck. He did not stink, unless one came very close and had an aversion to the most popular domestic cleaning fluid on the market.

And his face set it all off with a splendid tuck-shop simper, straight out of the pages of *Magnet*. Here I am, it said, a literary gentleman on a nice day out who knows that there is, indeed there is, such a thing as a free lunch.

In the cab, he had wanted to know about the rivalries and jealousies he assumed existed between professional models at a worse pitch than in any other business, including the theatre. It was inconceivable that beautiful young women competing for the same job should not want to scratch each others' eyes out. Did they ever get to actual fighting, eh? Pulling the hair, that sort of thing? Like the lacrosse team and all that?'

'No, no,' said Jessica. 'It's not a bit like that.'

'Come now,' he said. 'Don't think you're telling tales out of school.'

'But it isn't. We're not catty with each other, really not. That just shows how little idea you have of what goes on. It isn't like that, and you mustn't make it so.'

Kingsley did not like to be contradicted. He looked out of his nearside window, with a pout. The mere fact that Jessica had once been a mannequin, as he was still inclined to call it, did not give her the licence to override what he knew to be his own insights.

Jessica had not then decided upon her scheme, although every piece of nonsense that came from him showed her what a farce his 'big project' was likely to be.

'You see, when you are a model, and your looks, your body is the equivalent of your working capital, you kind of – well, specialize in one sort of appearance, one special look.' She wondered why she was bothering to explain, because the silly, petulant old fraud was still pouting through the window. 'Every other girl has something different. There's no point in resentment. I mean, every other girl seems to have the one thing you *don't* have – '

'Ah! You see!'

Jessica looked at him. He thought he had scored a point, so his face was once again wreathed in smirks. She felt the urge to reach across and pull at the end of his nose.

'There's no way,' she said, as coldly as she could, 'you or any other man will ever willingly understand what it is you make women think of their own bodies.'

'We make? *I* make? What sort of nonsense is this, Jessica?'

'Beyond-you sort, Uncle Maurice.'

Kingsley looked out of the cab window again. If his teddy bear had (so to speak) addressed him in such a fashion, he would have given it a good spanking. He glared at a goggled motorcyclist who had suddenly come up alongside in the stalled Regent Street traffic: a messenger from the nether regions, weaving between the slow streams.

Time is running out, he reflected. There is not much left to trickle through from the top bowl to the bottom one. He thought of the elegancies of his Occasional Piece on the hourglass he pretended to have seen on the market stall. Ah, words; ah, time; ah, me. He turned back to the lovely, long-legged niece he had always relished as by far the most attractive of his long-since scattered, abandoned or deceased family, willing to be conciliatory. Let her talk tosh if she wanted. There was the smoked salmon to think of. And the Nuits St Georges.

'Of course, if you'd had the good fortune to be sent into this ugly old world with the skin of an angel and a heavenly shape to match,' he said, showing his yellow teeth and looking at her knee, 'as you most certainly were, little Jessie – well, then!'

'Well then, what?'

'Well, then, it's obvious, isn't it, dear girl,' he beamed, confirming what he sought to refute. 'The roses are strewn at your dainty feet. All the doors of the kingdom are opened for you. Except the one into the gents, of course.'

Jessica fixed her attention on the notice in the back of the cab. THANK YOU FOR NOT SMOKING, it said. One of the latest ways of using weasel words. And for not burning, she thought, congratulating herself on her restraint.

Now, almost three years later, she could remember every word he had said. Sometimes, indeed, she thought she could remember every word every man had ever said to her. Words which could not be torn up into little pieces, and stuffed back down the throats which had delivered them.

Slippery fishes!

8

Blackeyes unscrewed the silvered cap from the bottle and shook out some of the amber lotion on to the tips of her fingers. The Sleepy Lagoon music was playing again, and it became like an ache at the back of her eyes. She would henceforth always remember this syrup of a waltz with a slow, viscous drip of melancholy.

The stuff felt tacky on her fingers.

She began to rub and then smooth or caress it into the top of her arm. The small circles slowly widened as she moved her fingers with what seemed an increasingly erotic deliberation towards her shoulder and her neck. Her head tilted back a little as she worked the slightly gooey dribbles of liquid into her skin, which meant that she could no longer see the shadowed faces of the men seated on the far sides of the room.

These faces were showing signs of sexual yearning, and, in some cases, torment. Fog at the window, fall in the air, a stuffy room, and a succession of bikini-clad young women had somehow deadened the emotions and yet quickened the senses: or, at least, the one sense they usually thought about the most. None of the previous girls had drawn from them quite so powerful a longing.

'Blackeyes willowed a little at the hips as her emptied-out thoughts picked up and clung to the thread of the saxophone. She followed it past a shingle of violins and on out into the deepest part of the sea. She was moving amongst the fishes and the waving fronds, I am a mermaid, whispered the music at the edge of her mind. I am a mermaid, said her own thoughts in echo, as she suddenly remembered a picture book with big clean white margins that she had once been given as a child.'

'He's left out the fucking coral,' said Jessica, who did not fail to notice the repeated, antique plural.

41

Blackeyes was soothing and smoothing a sticky dribble of the amber lotion down from her neck to the first swell of her breasts. Jamieson, staring into the dazzle around her, could feel moisture on his upper lip, but he did not want to creak his chair by reaching down into a pocket for his handkerchief. Nobody dared to move.

She hooked a finger into the top part of her bikini. Her small undulations came to an end. Her long stare sought out Jamieson.

Do it! urged his head, his loins, and the glint on his glasses. *Go on, do it!*

Blackeyes held herself very still, like one of those cut-out figures of a holiday girl that used to stand on the pavement outside the pharmacist's. In the sheening light her remarkable eyes looked, now, to be made of some black mineral. Her skin shone where residues of the sticky lotion lay unabsorbed on its surface.

One, two, she counted to herself, leaving her lips slightly parted. One, two, three, she counted again.

O My Darling, O My Darling
O My Darling Clemen-

She pulled down the top of her bikini. A sight that was almost a shudder of release went up from the seated humps. Her nipples had spoken to them. Have we got the job? they asked. Yes, we've got the job, they said. The tacky ooze trickled towards them: the oil of anointment.

And never mind the coral, Jessica added, with no trace of a smile, stranded on the jagged reef that encircled the fiction.

9

'Luncheon in a decent restaurant with a small menu, well-spaced tables, attentive waiters without anxiety or impertinence in their eyes, and a handsome young woman on the other side of your own stretch of pristine white linen is one of the most amiable of all pleasures of the flesh. An immediate gratification of the appetite is accompanied by the piquant sauce of even richer possibilities to follow the last of the wine . . .'

Kingsley could fetch up the great majority of his babblingly discursive Occasional Pieces word for word, including the ones which had not been picked for display between hard covers. Musings and posturings, ambles and rambles, bringings-to-mind, by-the-ways, diaphanies and epiphanies, reveries, valedictions and celebrations, all in a style that had been washed away by the acid rain. What, now, was a Man of Letters to do except clasp his teddy bear to his bosom and remember the delicious subordinate clauses of yesteryear?

Hoovering down his pallid starter of smoked salmon, Kingsley chewed upon his former 'reflections'. He was always ready to regurgitate them into quotation, stopping any conversation stone cold dead. The 'richer possibilities' had seldom become actual, even in what he remained willing to call the dear dead days. On this occasion, of course, with Jessica on the other side of the pristine white linen, consanguinity made them out of the question.

By God, though, she was a fine figure of a young woman. Look at the way her frock clung around her. A trifle hard in the eyes, perhaps. Often the case nowadays. Even bloody shop-girls had taken to answering back, and if you pinched someone's bottom, apparently, a prosecution was more than likely to follow.

Momentarily dispirited, he slowed his chewing jaws, and tried to concentrate his faltering attention on Jessica's slender arms and hands.

'The piquant sauce of even richer possibilities,' he said, suddenly.

'What?' asked Jessica, surprised, for she had been talking.

'To follow the last of the wine.'

'Uncle Maurice. What are you talking about? Are you listening to me – ?'

'Of course I am,' he said, mustering the pretence of indignation.

'Well, then. You can see what I mean. You can't really disagree.'

She knew he had not taken in a word for several minutes as he drifted off into whatever slow and weed-infested backwater he probably called a reverie.

'Mmm,' he said cautiously, almost in his Literary Voice. He was tempted to add Things Are Never Quite So Simple As One Supposes, which usually fitted the bill when this sort of thing happened.

'Uncle Maurice. You are a total fraud.'

He was alarmed by the lack of banter in her face and in her voice, and simpered a mild disclaimer.

They ate in silence for a while, helped by a waiter who topped up their glasses.

This is one of the bad things about going out, he mused as he poked without relish at his plate. You had to pay attention to other people. They caught you out when the thoughts you presumed to be safe and snug somehow got out between your lips.

In the same silence, with the evidence of his feebleness in front of her, Jessica saw the first outlines of her plan drift into view across the plates and glasses and pale old eyes.

'What was it you were saying, Jessie?'

She seemed to relent, probably because he had sounded so old and so plaintive. Nearly always worked, that. Even with the bloody shop-girls.

'The models. The other models,' she said, consciously lightening her voice. 'You said they were bound to be catty with each other. But if you genuinely want to know about these things. And I hope you do, Uncle, if – '

'Oh, I do. Really I do.'

He wondered whether they put as much smoked salmon on the plate as they used to do, and why it no longer tasted as nice as before.

' – like china-doll eyes when your own are too something else,' she was saying as he stopped his thoughts wandering again. 'Silkier hair, maybe. Or longer legs, more slender thighs. As I said – it's your working capital . . .'

'Or bigger titties,' he added, now fully attentive.

'What?'

'For example.'

He heard one of her long, painted fingernails ping against the rim of her wine glass, and caught the swath of her look across the table at him.

'Be fair now, Jessie,' he said, nervously. 'I was simply imagining myself in the situation you're talking about.'

'Imagining yourself as a *man* in that situation, you mean.'

'I can be no other.'

He knew that that sounded dignified, and wondered why she laughed. Still, it wasn't a hostile laugh, not one of those jeering kinds. Perhaps they were going to hit it off, after all.

'Then perhaps you should write your book,' she said.

'Of course I should! And of course I will. I don't want to pick your brains (you haven't got any, said his tone), but I do want to raid the larder. Your experiences. The things you saw happen. That sort of thing, eh?'

He noticed a waiter hovering, ready to take the plates away. There was a delicate little matter to be broached, and it was encouraging to see that Jessica was in fairly good humour. Perhaps I should write my book? Of course I should write my book! First things first, though. Wait for the bouncy little wop to do the clearing up . . .

'It's very good of you to take me out to lunch like this,' he

45

began, the waiter out of earshot. 'I suppose you – ah – not that it matters – ah – '

'You suppose what, Uncle?'

'Successful girl like you – '

'Yes?'

'Well. Use a credit card, do you? I expect.'

'Not necessarily,' she said, with a dry precision.

Kingsley sipped at his wine, as though for the first time, and broadcast an appreciative smack of the lips. He believed, with Hazlitt, that it was insipid to hint what you feel in a dumb show, but 'making a toil of pleasure' if you have to explain it. There was a pitch somewhere in between. He looked half-covertly around the place, and lowered his voice.

'Only, if you are paying in cash – *that* antiquated commodity – actual money, I mean – '

'Yes?' she prompted again, but knowing what he was about.

'Well. I was wondering. A little antique of me, too, of course. But – ah – '

'Don't worry.'

'Oh, I'm not *worried*, my dear – '

'I'll pass it across.'

She watched him with a close interest. A quiver of furtive satisfaction passed across his features, followed by a fugitive anxiety.

'Discreetly,' he said.

'Discreetly,' she agreed.

Kingsley twirled the stem of his glass, considered the matter, and sighed a martyr's sigh.

'It's unfortunate of course. One's sensibilities can be a bit of a burden, Jessica.'

'How do you mean?'

'Being trapped, I mean. In the customs and the civilities of the dear dead days. The moth-eaten and, yes, yes, eminently mockable prejudices of my generation. It all boils down to a question of respect, y'see. That's what it is, at heart.'

Jessica pretended to be obtuse.

'Age before youth, do you mean?'

'Oh. Yes. Yes, of course there's that too,' he blinked at her, puzzled. 'But I'm talking about something else. Respect for women. I am talking about the way to treat a lady.'

She controlled a chirrup of hilarity.

*

'I'm going back quite a while now. It was my first audition,' Jessica said, further on in her plan, and across another table. 'There was this rather oddly shaped bottle on the table made entirely of glass. It had a mirrored top. The table, I mean. It looked as though it were floating.'

Kingsley was enjoying himself. His niece was as delightful and as considerate as he had ever hoped. The details she was providing came thick and fast, like blossom falling in a wind. He believed that his powers of concentration were actually increasing now that he once again had something big to work on. But the bottle on the glass table made him think of *Alice in Wonderland,* and his attention strayed.

'What is the phrase our American cousins use when they are astonished?' he asked, in the middle of one of her sentences. 'Something blasphemous and scatalogical.'

Jessica did not want to be interrupted. She found it more congenial to be a narrator than she had expected, ordering sequences from her own life in a way that drained them of pain, and yet allowed them to wriggle deeper and deeper into her consciousness.

'What do you mean?' she frowned.

'Design. I'm talking about bloody designers. Did you ever read my piece on designers? Give something as decent and as ordinary as a table to one of those fellows and you'd throw up, wouldn't you, rather than sit down and eat at it.'

He mistook her expression, imagining that she disliked 'throw up' while she had food in her mouth.

'Go on,' he said, after apologizing. 'This is exactly the sort of detail I need. I don't stumble across this sort of thing very often, you know.'

Jessica watched him refill his wine glass, and felt, suddenly, a downward plunge into melancholy.

'Uncle Maurice. What is the point?'

'What is the point of what? Life, do you mean? Random molecules, dear girl. There is no point.'

She watched him refill his mouth. A fleck of veal strayed on his lip. Dead calf, she thought. The slaughter of babies.

'Holy shit!' he said suddenly, and beamed. 'That's what the Yanks say when they are astonished. That's what I was trying to recall. Holy shit! Rather graphic, don't you think – what's the matter, Jessica?'

She looked like someone who had just seen an evil spirit. Whatever it was sucked the blood from her face, and scooped deep down into the tunnels of her eyes. And then the blanched surprise turned back on itself to become a formidable hatred.

Kingsley twisted his head around to make sure that he was not the object of such venom. Behind him, a couple were being shown to a table. The man was fleshily marooned in his late fifties, but the accompanying young woman could hardly have reached her twenties. He had his hand cupped at her elbow, ostensibly to guide her through the tables, but the grasp was unmistakably proprietorial. The girl, Kingsley appreciated, was a corker.

'Good heavens, Jessie,' he said, turning back to his own table. 'Why are you looking like that? Who is it? Adolf Hitler or Jack the Ripper, or what?'

He did not yet know they were to be the tragic heroine of his book and one of her slayers.

'Eat your veal, Uncle,' Jessica said.

10

Soft folds of summery dusk came out of the head and began to fall across the park, tingeing the idle sounds of leisure with sadness. People released from the aquatint at the limit of memory were strolling about on the paths and on the grass. A few figures around the pond threatened to become mere silhouettes and then took on finer shades, more particular movements. Paper kites climbed higher and higher in the darkening sky and little boats skewed or bobbed on the darkening water. Silvery chimes came at the quarter from the palace. Beyond the park, bright rectangles splashed out light at the big new hotel overlooking the trees.

Not all the details were in place. These were a few selected out of an enormous number of other possibilities. But for all of them, there was an ache at the back of the sky, a tingle of nerves behind the shapes, a cry beyond the sounds. Memory still waited recovery beyond any one sequence of recollection. The smallest flicker at the limits of effort yielded up yet more inaccessible layers of loss and despoliation.

Here, now, a gleam on the surface of the reflecting materials which fenced off one time from another, a toy sailing boat caught a wayward eddy from the distant trees, and dipped, and veered. A small girl on the far side of the pond laughed. The sound hung for a moment, in the air, and became threatened before it fell back again into Jessica's striving mind.

She knew the nature of the threat, whereas the little girl did not.

It thickened and hunched around her, and picked up other sounds, other shapes. Trundle, trundle, trundle went the metal rollers. The body of the black-haired, dark-eyed beauty loomed into view.

'I know this isn't a very pleasant thing to have to do, sir, not

49

one little bit,' the policeman was saying, 'but if you would be so kind and helpful as to look at the young lady.'

The intrusion was too violent, and Jessica pushed it away. It could come later, in the proper place, if it came at all.

Let the small girl laugh. Let the sound not hang in the air.

'Uncle Maurice! Uncle Maurice!' she was calling. 'Come this side! It will come on this side!'

The little sailing boat was already within the reach of a grown-up's stretching arm, if only he would come and get it. But the arty gentleman with the floppy bow tie and kindly twinkle did not seem to be paying attention. He was looking the other way, past the old woman in a black hat who was feeding the birds, and across to the brighter and brighter lights of the hotel.

How irritating!

*

The restaurant at the top of the hotel was elevated in price as well as view. Kingsley had never eaten there, but he had stood in the park and sneered at it a few times.

'I don't know whether your palate agrees with mine or not,' he was saying, becoming Jamieson, leaning in with a slightly damp face, 'but I think you will be very much taken with the hint of violets on the nose and cherry stones on the tongue. This one is just beginning to drink nicely.'

He waited for what he expected to be a timid and respectful smile of pleasure. It did not come. Steady, dark eyes glowed back at him.

'Is it?' Blackeyes asked, expressionless.

'Well. Go on. Taste it.'

She picked up the glass, her long fingers bare of any adornment, but sensual in even the simplest act.

'I know nothing about wine.'

'Then we must see what we can do about changing that, mustn't we?' he smirked, watching the bow of her lips at the rim. 'Well? What do you think?'

She put her glass down, and looked at him.

'I know nothing about wine,' she said, in the same tones as before.

Jamieson took the lack of expression and absence of warmth as an unspoken but not unexpected question. One which he did not want to answer.

'You scarcely tasted it,' he said, no longer smiling. 'You hardly moistened your pretty lips. Go on, drink! That's the first thing you do if you want to find out more.'

She picked up her glass again, dutifully, and sipped a little more of the Charmes Chambertin as slowly or as deliberately as one might in a dream. He waited. His exasperation grew.

'Well?' he said, eventually.

'Are you married?'

'Is that any of your business – ?'

He stared at her, offended, but she did not look away.

'Now, look here,' he said, in a would-be straightforward tone. 'I want you to know something It is important to me that you know this. I want you to understand that I don't make a habit of this sort of thing. This is an out-and-out, utter exception, my making personal contact in this way. I always make a complete separation between my business life and my private life.'

'Do you have two key-rings?'

He could not decide whether this was irony or an unfamiliar slang or some other form of joke. She might be being sardonic: she might be utterly stupid. Her glittering black eyes gave him no clues.

'Yes,' he said, with a temporizing smile. 'I have two key-rings.'

She nodded such a serious nod that he thought, Jesus Christ! to himself.

A quintet of musicians began to play one of his least favourite tunes, behaving like extras in the kind of movie he never wanted to see. Unless he could throw off the mood of fretful discontent that had blown across from the darkened park towards him, the whole carefully planned evening was going to end in disappointment and detumescence.

51

He reached across the table, showing a width of white cuff and a subdued glimmer of gold. His hand overlaid hers, but he did not squeeze.

'You happen to be the first and only one of the models used by the agency we – listen, you are the first one I've so much as looked twice at. Outside working hours, I mean.'

She did not have to say thank you, but he did expect her to say something. Even a shift or signal in her black eyes would have represented token reward. But she said nothing, and her face said nothing.

Jamieson removed his hand.

'We are in for a chatty evening, clearly,' he said, and gripped the tall stem of his glass as though he intended to break it off.

She watched him drink. It was while the wine was half-way down his throat that she spoke, with as little apparent interest or animation as before.

'I don't have orgasms,' she said.

Some of the hint-of-violet really did reach his nose, but backwards, and some of the hint-of-cherry-stones drenched the protesting coil of his windpipe. He coughed and wheezed in helpless pain, trying not to discharge the remainder of his mouthful in a humiliating splatter across the table.

'Can I get you anything, sir?' a waiter asked, on the move, as Jamieson whooped, gasped and spluttered.

'A glass of water,' Blackeyes said, calmly.

She looked across at the musicians, because she liked the piece they were playing.

11

Maurice James Kingsley had all but completed his dressing on the morning he had so puzzlingly set his alarm clock. He had peed an orange and stinging torrent into the already soiled sink – following, as he always pointed out to himself, the precedent established by one of the greatest English poets of the century – and then switched on his wireless set for the enjoyable miseries of the news on the hour.

' – the operation for a transurethral resection of the prostate,' the uninvolved radio voice was saying. 'Our medical correspondent reports that this enables the prostate to be removed with an electric wire loop that is inserted through the urethral opening . . .'

How disgusting the news is, he thought. Nobody is going to shove an electric wire loop through *my* urethral opening.

'. . . At home the death has been announced of the novelist, critic, and broadcaster Hazel Prosperi. A member of this year's Booker Prize Committee, she was perhaps best known for her many appearances on – '

Kingsley heard no more for at least a minute. He had jumped out of his swivelling chair with the alacrity of a man half his age, but now stood very still, tingling at the scalp, his face changing colour.

'My God,' he whispered.

And then joy burst through all his limbs. It even reached the urethral opening. Torrents of exultation rode upon his thin blood, and swept so strongly into his thin, old arms that he raised them above his head, clenching and unclenching his hands in noisy triumph.

'Glory!' he cried. 'Glory! Glory! Hallelujah!'

His eyes roved wildly around the huge, shabby attic, as though he were seeking a physical manifestation of his joy beyond the limitations of his elderly frame. He found it in the teddy bear, arse-up on the disarranged bed. A sight that enabled him to abandon evangelical fervour for the equal comforts of his Literary Voice.

'"How fresh, O Lord, how sweet and clean are thy returns,"' he boomed, rolling each word from tongue to teeth like a boiled sweet in his mouth, and rushing to the teddy.

He gathered the careworn little creature into his arms, and kissed it so enthusiastically that its patchy fur was made wet, so that both of them seemed to be dribbling with delight.

Around and around the room they went, in a dance of joy that made the mostly bare boards groan and creak. Kingsley held out the teddy's left arm so that it was in approximately the right position for a dimly remembered Palais foxtrot, but the tune soon trickled out of his head, as the spasm of energy removed itself from his limbs.

'Dead meat,' he panted, the whirl finished, and the knee trouble beginning. 'She's dead meat.' He waited for his breath to come back, holding the teddy bear limply at his side by one of its fat little brown arms.

'Pushing up the daisies,' he said, in a more normal voice, before switching off the radio, whose announcement needed to be supplemented in ampler and more accurate terms.

'A member of this year's Booker Prize Committee,' he boomed, 'she was perhaps best known for her infamous and as she then thought anonymous attack in *The Times Literary Supplement* of 18 September 1953, on the elegant and perceptive *Occasional Pieces Again* by Maurice James Kingsley, probably England's most – ah – most – '

He did not reveal the precise nature of the accolade he was about to award himself, for the boom went out of his voice, and the wildness left his eyes.

'Poor old thing,' he whispered, after a while. 'Poor scruffy, scraggy, silly old bitch.'

Scratching around in his stock of remembered verse for a marginally more suitable valediction, or a less colloquial one, and for once finding nothing, he had a sudden and sharp sense of how dreadful it was to lose an almost lifelong enemy. It was even worse than when Edith Sitwell flew away for good to the far bank, on the back of a sick crow.

He was disconcerted by the dampness at his eyes, and pulled the dangling teddy back against his chest, in search of comfort.

'Not many of us left, eh?' he said as he hugged it. 'The far door keeps opening an inch or two wider, my little chickadee. We shall soon be trudging through it ourselves. You know that, don't you? But thank God for you, my faithful little darling – '

Bzzzzzzz.

The grating buzz of the entryphone cut into the maudlin excess. He went stiff with fear, holding his breath, and hoping that what was to him a terrible sound would not be repeated.

Bzzzz – zzz – zzzzzz.

No doubt about it, someone, something, was pressing his bell in the street far below, demanding access.

'Oh, Christ,' he said, letting out the air in a whistle of dread.

Bzzzz – zzzz – zzzzzz.

Extraordinarily flustered, Kingsley bore the teddy bear back to his rumpled bed, hissing at it.

'Just you shut up, you hussy,' he warned. 'Hide your bloody self, and don't move an inch! Quick! Quickly! Quickly!'

He heaved up a tangle of bedding and covered the teddy, completely. The entryphone continued to buzz, in longer-held sequences. Could it be the spirit of Hazel Prosperi already abroad, wielding weapons far worse than a rolled-up copy of *The Times Literary Supplement*? No one called on him unannounced nowadays, except the amorphous terrors of obscure accusations from his tormented imagination.

At first sight, too, it could indeed have been one such as these which clicked and hummed and fidgeted on the wide, worn-down stone steps at the street door, but the figure there was actually far more harmless than it would have liked to be.

'C'mon. C'mon. C'mon,' Mark Wilsher fumed, unable to keep still.

He kept his thumb going on and off one of a battery of buttons set at the side of a pair of paint-peeling doors.

A proliferation of trade names on the ill-kept Edwardian building showed it to be one of the many places in the street given over to the wholesale fashion business. A majority of the names was oddly aggressive, revolutionary, or anarchist, though the trade, of course, was ruthlessly and classically capitalist.

Mark was dressed on the cutting edge of young male fashion, or, as he might have termed it, state-of-the-art scaf. He regarded himself as a New Journalist. Older members of the same disreputable pseudo-profession would have vented their contempt in roughly similar terms by calling him a new kind of journalist, without the capitals.

A rack of blouses rattled by on metal castors on the pavement behind him, just as an elderly and already barely audible voice issued at last from the entryphone grille. 'Who is it?', it said, or Mark, deafened, presumed it to say.

'This is Mark Wilsher here,' he announced, with the smallest pause at his name, as though to allow anyone hearing it for the first time enough space to fall backwards in astonishment. 'KRITZ magazine. To see Maurice James Kingsley.'

He spoiled the effect by adding a much less confident 'OK?'

'Who is pressing my bell?' came a faint, dry wind out of the hole in the wall.

'This is Mark Wilsher, of KRITZ magazine – '

'I am not at home to trades people.'

Chrisalm'ee, Mark muttered, and tugged in anxious frustration at his single ear-ring. He leant in closer to the grille, as though about to spit in it, and shouted up the name of the magazine again, omitting his own.

'Identify yourself, or leave me alone!'

Feeble, distant and distorted though it was, the panic in the voice was obvious. Mark could not understand what was happening. Was he to remain puzzled and unadmitted on the pitted stone step, shouting his identity into the wall?

On the top floor, Kingsley had hung up his entryphone as though it were a needle-toothed creature to be put back in a bag. He could make no sense of the clatterings and shoutings from the street, beyond the possibility that someone was abusing him in German.

'*Someone* might have been due to call, petal,' he said, still spinning alarm as he looked at the bed where the teddy bear lay hidden. 'But who? Why? What? Is that why I put the alarm on this morning? Eh? I'll tell you one thing, I have no business with a bloody Hun, have I?'

He stopped his nervous pacing, and cocked his head to listen, willing the buzzer to be silent. But the entryphone grated again. Coincidentally, a police car let off its siren in the street below, and the two harsh let-me-in and let-me-pass sounds folded into each other, urgency upon urgency. The combination ignited an orange flare in the old man's head.

'I have done nothing wrong,' he moaned. 'My hands are blameless '

The siren receded in an urban howl, but the bell would not stop its angry buzz. He put his blameless hands tight against his ears.

'They're coming for you,' the teddy bear informed him in the muffled, little-girl voice of his niece. 'They've found out about it at last!'

'Shut up!' he shouted, and then lowered his hands in a trembling flutter, acknowledging more than his foolishness.

Down below, one of the double doors opened, to evacuate an anorexic with green and vermilion reefs of hair, kohl-puddled eyes, and the matt-white face of a troubled clown. She was carrying a stack of flat cardboard boxes in her matchstick arms. She glared so fiercely at Mark that he took his thumb off the button.

'Vishusvampentcha!' she spat.

'Nah,' said Mark, who was up to this.

'Comfertheboxes.'

'Nah.'

'Now look – !'

'Comfer Maurice Kingsley.'

'Oo?'

'Yeh.'

'Notvishusvampdenentcha?' she asked, looking up and down

57

the pavement. 'Where the bleed'nell are they, den?'

'Late?'

The punky, skinny girl looked at him. Now that it was established that he was not from Vicious Vamp, a lingerie house favoured by middle-aged housewives, he began to emerge as an authentic umanbeein.

'Who this bloke?' she asked, modifying the patois.

'Lives here. His pad here, ri?'

'Whatshedoden?'

'Wri'er. You know.'

She stared out of twin ditches of kohl, then screwed up her little face in disgust.

'Im!'

'Yeh? Like that?'

'Watch your pinkie!'

'Yeh?' he frowned.

'Wrinkly, ri?'

'Tha's ri,' he confirmed. 'Hearse case.'

'Nu'er!' she exclaimed, continuing to economize with any middle consonants.

'Yeh?' Mark said, getting more concerned.

'Right up the top,' she nodded back at the open door.

'Ta,' he said, giving her an appreciative once-over. 'Yeh. Well.'

They held their appraisals, briefly, mutually approving each other's garb, each other's youth, each other's speech, then she swept on past him, giving the cardboard boxes a hoist. Both had communicated volumes of information and rafts of comment in the complicated and exhausting brevities of their exchange.

As he went in through the double doors, she was already screeching at some unfortunate idler further along the street who might have been the tardy Vicious Vamp, but by then her noise had become incomprehensible, even to Mark. He hitched up his shoulders as he passed over the threshold into a tired but tiled entrance lobby, girding himself to meet a monster.

But Kingsley, high above him, was still enduring a worse anxiety. He was standing as still as he could in the middle of his litter of space, addressing himself in terms which failed to work.

'Calm. Calm. Stay calm. I am innocent. I have done nothing. Calm. Calm. Stay calm.'

> O My Darling, O My Darling
> O My Darling Clementine –

The tinkle could have come from the bed where the teddy bear was in a rebellious mood under a heap of grubby bedclothes, or it could have come from Jessica, or his own head, or some other smart-arse setting himself up as judge and jury and executioner.

'Calm. Calm. Stay calm. I am innocent. I have done nothing. Calm. Calm. Stay calm.'

The front door into his room began to bang. They or It had come for him: the moment he most feared this side of the pains of his own death throes. He sucked in his breath, as though taking in the last available portion of air.

Bang! Bang! Bang!

Kingsley shrugged, with a startlingly sudden self-possession. His demons receded back into the walls, or the past. He padded across to the door, and pulled the poker-sized bolt.

'Mr Kingsley – ? Yeh?' the accusing, out-of-breath apparition said.

The fuddled old man peered bravely out at the baggily clothed, spiky-haired and silver-eared young man. No, no, this could not be the thing called Nemesis. He straightened, and drew out of himself the fruity dignities of a forgotten actor-manager in his prime.

'Maurice James Kingsley himself,' he announced. 'At Home. But only by appointment.'

'Fair enough, squire.'

'Who are you, young man? What do you require of me?'

Mark was staring at the unkempt old man as he might have done at a grisly exhibit come to life in the London Dungeon. The impression threatened greater authenticity when a dust-hung strand of abandoned cobweb lightly touched him on the brow. Mark brushed it away, and took half a step backwards.

'*KRITZ*,' he said, in a way that left no doubt about the capital letters.

'What – ?'

'Mark Wilsher. *KRITZ* magazine. Yeh?'

'*KRITZ*?' asked Kingsley, puzzled, and putting the title back into the lower case.

'Magazine.'

They stared at each other again, mutually on guard. The displaced cobweb swung between them, riding a current of air from the stairs.

How can a bloke like this have written a book like that? italicized into Mark's thoughts. Once there, the sentence would be difficult to dislodge.

Kingsley smacked the butt of his hand into his forehead, grotesquely exaggerating a belated gust of recollection.

'Good gracious me!' he exclaimed, and smacked his head again. 'Angels and ministers of grace defend us!'

'Come again?'

'My dear chap! I do humbly beg your pardon! The arrangement had completely slipped my mind.'

'That's all right. Don't knock yourself out.'

Kingsley did not permit the swirl of recollection to move him from the doorway, where he remained in a way that effectively blocked entry. Mark was not now sure that he wanted to go in anyway, but he tried to peer around the old man into the cave beyond.

'The explanation, you see, if by any chance you are at all interested,' Kingsley boomed, just stopping short of placing his hand more gently upon his brow, like a Rodin figure, 'is that you have broken in, so to speak, upon a wingèd flight of reverie. On the perilous ridge I hung alone, if you follow me.'

Mark swallowed a guffaw, and made an apologetic gesture.

'There it is, there it is. "With what strange utterance did the loud dry wind Blow through my ear !" Hence my obtuseness, sir. Ah, the word. The word, my boy!'

'There you go,' said Mark.

'How civility and the discourse of the mundane hour suffers

at its voracious insistence! But you, young man, you are my visitor from Porlock, eh?'

Mark vaguely recognized the overworked allusion, but he did not want to encourage any more of this nonsense.

'No. *KRITZ*,' he said, with a parodied wink.

Kingsley frowned, unsure whether he was being made fun of, then decided not. He had invoked both the loud dry wind and *Kubla Khan*'s interrupter so many times without receiving either correction or abuse that he had learnt to misinterpret the boredom or the disdain on the faces of his listeners. Stepping aside, he gave one of his equally well-practised *fin-de-siècle* (*soi-disant*) sweeps of the arm.

'My abode beckons. Come you in, fellow-me-lad. And welcome!'

Mark hesitated, then slid cautiously around Kingsley, remembering the girl's warning to watch out for his pinkie. Once inside the attic, he stopped in surprise and gaped from corner to corner. His mouth opened, and a strange light jumped into his eyes: one that Kingsley could not fathom.

The 'beckoning abode' he was dimly aware lacked order and cleanliness and many of what some people seemed to regard as the basic comforts.

'The powerhouse. The pump-room, old chap,' he said, more defensively than the fruity tones could accommodate. 'It may not be all that it might be, but it is the arena, sir, for all my muses and imaginings.'

Mark let out a long, soft whistle.

'What is the matter?' Kingsley asked, peering nervously at the young man.

'Terrific,' Mark said, extending each syllable.

Kingsley looked around the room, trying to see it with fresh eyes, and failing. His visitor meanwhile continued to make other barely comprehensible sounds, apparently of praise. Kingsley recognized the words 'digital' and 'fierce', but they appeared to be out of their normal context, let alone their normal meanings. He was relieved when the presumed praise

61

was confirmed with a final, emphatic, and understandable 'very nice place you've got here'.

This was enough of an invitation for the host to spread wide his arm again, but this time in the older gesture of a humble peasant scattering seeds on the fruitful earth. The full resonances of his Literary Voice came back to him with the movement, shades finer in pitch than the plausible but nevertheless heartfelt impersonation of the redundant actor-manager.

'"Joy,"' he declaimed, '"is the sweet voice, Joy the luminous cloud — We in ourselves rejoice! And thence flows all that charms or ear or sight, All melodies the echoes of . . ."'

12

Jessica, fixing her attention on the thief and plunderer, unravelled a remembered poetic rant. 'And thence flows all that charms or ear or sight,' he had said, splaying his hand, as they walked along a wet street. He had collided with a woman almost as old as himself, and spiked a young man in the eye with the umbrella. Her umbrella, of course, held so that he had most of the cover and she had most of the drips.

She went to the window to look down at the cobbled mews in which she lived. The window was open an inch or two. She leant into the small stir of air, city air, bearing foulness at its heart, but at this moment a cleansing waft.

'All melodies the echoes of me,' insisted her thoughts. 'Echoes of *my* voice, of my experiences, and of what he has stolen from *me*.'

It was not relevant that she had offered it in the first place.

She made her eyes settle on the fat white tubs of dying flowers on either side of the primrose-coloured door of the twee little house opposite. Such urban ineptitudes were mildly soothing, in a harmlessly melancholic twinge.

'Echoes of me,' her mind said, refusing to allow the diversion.

Jessica stared at the withering, saucer-like blooms in the white tubs, and she stared at the yellow door, and she stared at the cobblestones. These things were real, real, real. They possessed their differing solidities and textures, but they were real solidities, real textures. The materiality of things. She yearned for it. Autonomous identity.

'An echo,' said her echoing head, instead.

She had come to understand that women were so used to having their lives expressed in terms of male voices, male judgements, male desires, and the manipulative power of men, that they did not have the same hold on the substance of their beings as their oppressors had. But the loss and the confusion she was feeling at the partly opened window came from even deeper apprehensions of abuse.

Jessica's complicated plot had totally misfired.

And now she considered herself to be little more than words written by a sick old man. She was less than the drooping flowers in the tub, less than the yellow front door, less than the flinty stones, less than the glass in the window, the wood of the sill, and all that charmed or ear or sight. Full stop. A mark on the page: someone else's page. Full stop.

13

Blackeyes was still a novice, but she was getting many more jobs now. Her face and body gleamed down from the hoardings, advertising Lagoon. She had also acquired at least one 'friend' (with two key-rings) who had influence in the constellations where she wished to shine. At least, Jamieson was saying that he would do this and he would do that for her, always providing she learnt to groan and gasp beneath him. He may well have mentioned her name here and there.

Those who took especial notice of her said that she would not go so far as she might unless there were more animation in her face. She still seemed like one in the middle of a long, slow dance, hypnotized by some secret music.

But these observers, kindly or (as in most cases) not, did not give due account for the sensuality of the passive. Her perfectly formed oval of a face was a blank upon which male desire could be projected. Her luminous, large, jet-like eyes said nothing, and so said everything. She was pliable. She was there to be invented, in any posture, any words, over and over again, in ejaculatory longing.

Her lovely head, at this moment, was virtually enclosed by an aluminium box, of the kind used for very close shots of eyes and face in a photographer's studio. She was wearing an off-the-shoulder peasant blouse that had never been near a stook of corn.

'The young photographer,' Kingsley's narrative said, 'was a febrile type who has since become relatively famous in those sorts of tabloid columns where but to appear at all would more properly be described as a disgrace. He has learned, while acquiring such apparently welcome notoriety, how to stop prancing and jigging like a child who wants a wee-wee, how to adjust the spelling of his once wholly plebeian first name, and how to tell amusing stories about the risible gaucheries of young photographers that are in fact about himself, way back in the mists of his painful obscurity, in days such as this one.'

Blackeyes listened.

'Now all I want you to do until I say otherwise is to move your eyes, O-K?' the photographer was saying, moving about (as Jessica had better described it) as though he had a bad itch. 'Move them suddenly. Now slowly. Like those eyes on elastic bands in the old china dolls, know what I mean? Only your eyes. Got it, darling?'

'Got it.'

He stayed his prance to stand and contemplate her.

'You have extraordinarily beautiful eyes,' he said. 'And the shape of your face – Ah. Just one little thing, angel.'

Unnecessarily, he diverted the flow of her silky black hair by a millimetre, his stubby fingers lingering even more unnecessarily at her neck. He stepped back to examine her again, holding his head first to one side and then to the other like a cartoon thinker, simulating a wholly professional detachment.

'Funky fresh,' he said, delivering the verdict.

He waited for her to smile an acknowledgement. She didn't.

'Your face, Blackeyes. It's wonderful. From my point of view, yeh? I tell you, it's so – so – ' he searched for an appropriate word, without any intention of finding it. 'You see. A guy can run out of things to say. But your face, darling. Your big, black, beautiful eyes. They're going to take you all the way!'

This time he waited so long, and stared so hard, that he compelled an answer.

'Thank you,' she said.

'The fact of the matter is,' he went on, unreasonably encouraged, 'I don't think that I personally have ever seen such a perfect face. Oh, in paintings, maybe. Old paintings, know what I mean? The Virgin Mary sort of thing.'

He waited as long and looked at her as hard, but did not get even the previous minimal reward.

Virgin Mary, she was thinking.

'O-*kay*. Let's go. Let's magic it here. Put your hands on your knees, and forget all about them. Think face. *Be* face. I want you to be in front of your face looking at yourself behind your face seeing yourself looking at yourself.'

Virgin Mary, she was thinking.

'Got it, honey?'

'Got it.'

He began to take pictures at last, but continued to instruct her in a rapid, increasingly self-excited staccato. Look up. Look down. Look right. Look left. Click and flash and call, call and flash and click. No! Don't move your head, angel. Oh, funk-ee. Look left. Look right. Look down. Look up. Fan Tas Tic.

'I promise you,' he said, 'you've got a face that'd sell condoms in a convent.'

After a while, she was able to pick out the precise instruction and abandon the rest of what the Jumping Jack was saying. His enthusiasms sank down into their own burble. She was listening, within herself, to other sounds. But only Jessica knew this. It was the last thing Maurice James Kingsley would have her do, even when his quivers of fear sent up the orange flashes into his guilty head.

*

The toy shop claimed to be the biggest in London. The little girl thought it must be half as big as England itself. In this part of it, long rows of dolls sat on their frilly bottoms, with chubbily outstretched arms, between walls of dusty turquoise. An amplified 'music box' was tinkling out an electronic Clementine.

O My Darling, O My Darling
O My Darling Clementine

It seemed to take for ever and ever to walk alongside the crowded shelves. Blue-eyed and beribboned babies, one after the other, dressed in satin and lace.

You are gone and lost forever
Lost forever, Clementine

'That one!' she pointed, stiffening with excitement, and not daring to move her eyes.

'This one? Are you sure?'

The child detected what she thought was a note of disapproval in the questions. She could already taste disappointment, which was like a kiss from the man with the prickly face she was told she must call 'my new daddy'.

'That one. Oh, yes. That's the one. Please. Please, Uncle Maurice!'

'If you want it, my little chickadee, you shall have it. But you are sure that out of all these lonely little dollies who have no mummy this is the lonely little doll you really want?'

'Oh, yes! Yes! Yes!' she jigged, more sure now that she was going to get it.

'Ah, but what will you give me? Will you give *me* a big kiss? Or is it just for dolly?'

He stooped to offer her his cheek.

When he had been kissed, and had kissed, Uncle Maurice lifted the doll from the shelf. He held it up and away from her as joy took away her breath.

'You must call her Clementine,' he said, as severely as though she had done something naughty. There wasn't a twinkle in his eye.

'Why? Why?'

'Because that is the name of the little tune they are playing. Listen.'

He waited, his head nodding in time to the amplified tinkle-tinkle of the music, and then broke into song at the right moment.

'O My Darling,' he sang. 'O My Darling. O My Darling Clementine.'

She did not like the name. It was too long and it began with a harsh sound at the back of the mouth. But she also knew how easily nice things, wonderful things, could be taken away if she did not pay attention to what the grown-ups wanted. Her mother would bend to whisper and to smile into her ear, the curtains move and sigh at the window, and suddenly she was alone in the room. Behave. Be good!

'Yes. Clem-en-tine. All right.'

Uncle Maurice looked at her too evenly, and she felt a little jump of fear. The same kind she got at the turn of the stair, at the closing of the door, at the raised voices on the top landing.

'Clementine!' she exclaimed, and clapped her hands.

'Then it's time for her to say *your* name, too!' he said, smiling now, and tilting the doll forwards to the girl. Her arms opened wide to receive it.

Ma-ma went Clementine.

'Oh, it's crying, she's crying, poor little thing,' said Uncle Maurice.

She hugged and hugged the doll so that it would have no reason to cry, not ever. When she looked up, still rocking the new baby in her arms, she was surprised to see that the tears were in her uncle's eyes after all.

*

Out of the cavern, out of the canyon, tinkle-tinkle as remote as the sounds of a crushed flower, the burbling enthusiasms became clear again. From within an aluminium shine, she paid attention again.

' – on posters fifty feet high, angel, you'll see. So if you could try just a *leetle* more expression, mmm? Like you're about to make love, or – '

He stopped. His face and voice changed so completely that she wondered if the clenching pain in her stomach had shown on her face. A face that, during her young years, she had made into a mask that rarely lifted. There were no windows into her mind.

'Oh, I don't know. I don't know,' the photographer was saying. 'Something here is not – not – '

He walked up and down in front of her, up and down, turning his back and facing her and turning his back. The movements of a man imitating the movements of active pondering: 'I wonder,' he mused, out loud, in proof. 'I wonder. Mmm.'

He stood still again, and looked at her, long and hard.

'There's some sort of reflection happening here. There's a definite upshine, know what I mean? It's ruining what is in fact a very good set of head shots.'

He seemed about to begin his musing and his pacing, but then:

'Your blouse.'

Blackeyes stayed silent.

'Your blouse, Blackeyes. It's coming up from your blouse. I mean, that's why I said for you to wear off-the-shoulder in the first place. Skin don't reflect in the same way. But it *is* your bloody blouse, love. Would you believe it.'

Unhelpful, wordless, she kept her head as still as she had been instructed.

'I don't think we should compromise here, do you?' He pushed his sausage-like fingers into his tight curls. 'I mean, you don't get anywhere in this business by accepting second best.'

A bluebottle was bouncing and droning against the far window, trying to get out.

'Take it off,' he said.

'Sure.'

He watched her as she took off her blouse, moving her head clear of the box.

'You're a professional. You're going to go a long way. You've got the right attitudes as well as everything it takes.'

'Yes,' she said, listening to the fly.

'Oh, dear. Your bra. It's almost the same colour. Same colour, same problem. Do you think you could . . .?'

He could read her expression, and did not wonder why her big eyes flicked sideways to look at the window. By now, he was confident that she would do exactly as she was told: as confident as the imperious bulge in his tight jeans.

But she did not put her fingers to the back of his head when, a few minutes later, he stretched his face and leant in and took a nipple gently between his lips and then even more gently between his teeth.

70

Where has the fly gone? she wondered, for the somnolent buzz had stopped. It had started to crawl up the woodwork at the side of the window. Kingsley put it there because he always had a bluebottle in his fictions. The fly in the ointment, he called it, before pulling off its wings.

14

Mark Wilsher had plumped himself down into Kingsley's one good chair. He had a cassette recorder on the boards beside him. A small red eye glowed as the tape turned.

'In your book, Mr Kingsley, in *Sugar Bush*, in obviously crucial places, you sort of, sort of – Well. Put it this way. What I'm interested in here – crucially – is the sort of use you make, obviously, of fashion, the praxis, and how this relates to the emerging feminist consciousness, of, well, the use of women. Obviously.'

Kingsley was as much irritated by the strange young man's barbarous language as he was by the uninvited occupation of his swivel chair.

'Obviously,' he said.

'I mean this is where it's crucially mediating sexism and style, yes? A real dilemma being worked out, yes? I expect you've seen *KRITZ* magazine, Mr Kingsley, so you'll know obviously that these are the parameters we – '

'Obviously.'

The grating repetition made the young man stop.
'What?'

'I *think* I've seen it,' Kingsley boomed. 'Tucked in amongst all the other ordure on the newsagent's rack. The name rings a distant and cracked bell. But I cannot say that I've gone quite so far as *ac*tually *ob*viously to *purchase* a copy. Better by far if you assume my ignorance of it.'

Mark looked at him, and then swivelled in the chair.

'I'm picking up the wrong vibes here,' he said.

'You bet your bloody life you are.'

They considered each other, Mark creaking the chair, Kingsley breathing heavily. They could make nothing of the appraisal.

'My stance, Mr Kingsley, if you'll – my own thing here, is to make a sort of, a sort of synthesis between rock music, fashion, and literature.'

'Is such a thing possible?'

'They're all to do with *style*. Right?'

'Style,' said Kingsley, as though this were a new word in a phrase-book language course.

'You could say obviously it started with Glam Rock obviously and Gary Glitter, way back in the – '

'What?' Kingsley interrupted. 'Who?'

'Yeh, there you are. Old stuff.' Mark apologized, with an embarrassed swivel. 'But obviously it develops on from there, right? Into the temper of the times. The prevailing whatsit. So what we're about, what *I'm* specially into is – *what it is like.*'

'What what is like?'

Mark nodded towards the windows.

'Out there. What it is.'

Kingsley also looked towards the windows, pulling his lips together, and briefly sucking spittle through his teeth.

'That is my chair,' he said. 'You are sitting in my chair.'

'Right,' conceded Mark, looking around. 'Where do you want me to sit, then?'

'On your arse, sir. Or on your synthesis. I doubt whether they are fundamentally different.'

Mark snorted a wary amusement, but then decided that he owed it to himself to be offended. He reached down and jabbed at a button on the cassette recorder, and the little eye of red light blinked off.

'Jesus, man, where you at?' he said, not getting out of the chair. 'You should stop this enigmatizing. You're rapping like somebody who's never even heard of Peter York – !'

'Who?'

'I don't believe this.'

'Oh, the actor,' Kingsley frowned, offended. 'Of course I bloody well have.'

Mark barked a laugh compounded of despair and pity, further offending the old man, who sucked spittle between his teeth again as though he were about to gob it out in dismissive rhetoric. But then, as Mark blinked at him, ready to recoil, Kingsley seemed to go slack, inside and out. He looked, all at once, so worn and confused, and so pathetic, that Mark thought he must be on the point of death itself.

And it came to the young man, at that moment, the incandescent revelation. Maurice James Kingsley did not have the knowledge and did not have the language necessary for the composition of *Sugar Bush*.

Mark saw, then, the cloudy but approaching shape – so far, no bigger than a word-processor – of a literary scandal. Not one in the Hitler *Diaries* class, of course, but good enough for a few inside page columns in one of the nationals. Oh, if he were to be the one to uncover it!

'Mr Kingsley,' he began, cautiously treading the path through the blackthorn which seemed to be opening up before him. 'Who did you talk to for the background – um – stuff – I mean, are you personally acquainted with any models, or – ?'

He remembered that he had switched off the recorder, but before he could reach down to press the right button, the entryphone buzzed. An implosion of dread on the old man's face knocked the question out of Mark's mouth.

'Mr Kingsley – ?'

Kingsley did not hear him. Policemen were at the street door again, big feet growing out of the step, and stone also in their faces where their eyes should be.

Bzzzzz zzzz zzzz.

'That'll be the photographer,' Mark said. 'Are you all right?'

If this were going to be a real shudder and twitch cardiac arrest, he vowed as he rose from his chair, he was not going to give that old, loose-lipped, yellow-toothed mouth the kiss of life. No, sir.

And any normal person who was not anywhere near even the first sightings of his own middle age would have found Kingsley's demeanour incomprehensible. The old man had lived alone for more than fifty years, and during that time he had slowly lost most of his wish or his ability to adjust his face or his emotions for the benefit of any potential witness.

Talking within himself had spilled out into talking to himself, and this, in turn, deflected soliloquy into conversations with the teddy bear, a comfort preserved from a timid and neglected childhood. Anxieties which had once been mere flickers of spiritual unease, and guilts that had coiled up into a small tight bundle at the back of thought, now flared and unwound more readily than ever before.

'Hello?' Mark spoke into the entryphone, which felt sticky in his hand and made him hold back a shudder. 'Yeh. This is it. Right up the top. Lots of stairs, and there's no lift.'

The word 'photographer' had belatedly lodged itself in Kingsley's scrabbling head. The menacing policemen left the step, but they looked back over their blue-black shoulders as they went along the pavement, their faces leaking away into small blobs of white.

Kingsley shouted that he did not propose to have his picture taken.

'But it's all been set up.' Mark grinned at him. 'It's already been arranged.'

'No. I never have my portrait taken. I have not allowed it in years.'

'Oh, come on now. It's not for a Wanted Poster, is it, sir?'

Another strange spasm forked across the old man's face, and he backed himself against the peeling wall.

'This is a gross and unwarrantable breach of my – ' he began to shout.

'But I've let him in now, haven't I?'

'And you had no right! You ignorant and malformed little shit!'

'Hey,' said Mark. 'Hey.'

'Would you have intruded upon Proust in this manner?' Kingsley spluttered, out of control. 'Is this the way you would have banged in upon Henry James?'

'Who?' said Mark, meaning incredulity, not ignorance, but causing the old man to tremble like a butterfly on an aubretia.

'Let me tell you this – let me tell you – you – half-educated, undernourished – ah – ah – '

'Hey. Don't get crusty!'

' – ah – unsightly – ah – gobbet of – of – catarrhal snot, you – !'

The abuse could not be sustained, because a loud banging had started at the door into the room.

'That'll be him, then,' smirked the young man, as he moved to open it, his eyes not leaving Kingsley. 'They're going to put you on the cover, I think. You could be on your way to being a *cult*, Mr Kingsley. Try that on for size!'

'A cult?'

It was as swift a transformation as any variety theatre had ever seen, and astonishing enough to cause Mark to stop before he had opened the door.

'Worth a bit of bother,' he said, ignoring the irritable banging.

'Do you have a looking-glass of any kind?' Kingsley asked in a new voice, his hand already trying to flatten down the grey tufts on his head.

Mark grinned at him in further incredulity, more delight.

'And a comb, dear boy. If you possess such a thing.'

'Christ,' said Mark.

Still smoothing his scalp, and simpering ingratiatingly, Kingsley appeared oblivious to the picture he was giving. He straightened himself grandly, and flapped his hand, airily insouciant.

'"My genial spirits fail, And what can these avail,"' he intoned, nodding at the banging door, '"To lift the smoth'ring weight from off my breast?"'

Mark opened the door, to reveal a glowering near-clone of himself on the other side, burdened with equipment.

'Deaf in there, are you?' the clone growled. 'It's only me lugging all this up all them stairs, ennit?'

'How you going to do this, Colin?'

'How do you mean?'

'Quick is how I mean.'

'*How* do you mean?'

'I mean,' said Mark, with an unduly heavy emphasis, 'that

you won't be long about. I mean you'll be taking your couple of shots and leaving me to it, yeh?'

Colin dumped two shoulder bags, and only half-nodded at Kingsley.

'You're joking,' he said.

'I'm joking? How am I joking?'

The photographer nodded at Kingsley again, without seeing him.

'How do I know what I want till I hear what he says, what he is? Think I'm at the seaside, do you? Hanging on the railings of the bloody pier, giving little cards out. Is that it?'

The two young men were so preoccupied with each other that they had little mind for Kingsley, who was watching them nervously, his hands rising and falling in small, nervous flutters.

'Now listen, Colin – '

'No, you listen. I'm not having this. I'm not into put-downs from you.'

'An interview. This is an in-ter-view. OK?'

'Yeh. So?' Colin thrust out his neck.

'An interview', Mark responded, as though to a simpleton, 'is a one-to-one thing. It's a one-to-one symbiosis.'

'Ooooh,' said Colin, continuing to set up his tripod.

I've never been as well known as I should, Kingsley was thinking. Too polished, too allusive, too bloody good: what do you expect? I'll drink to that.

Muttering a little as his thoughts broke surface, he forgot about his visitors, and went to the meat-safe on the wall. He could not hope – as he had often said, with Coleridge – from outward forms to win the passion and the life, whose fountains are within. But that all depended on how the within got to be within in the first place, he acknowledged, as he unscrewed the cap on a half-bottle of Scotch. Cheers.

'I *told* Andrew, I mean I *told* him,' Mark was saying, with exaggerated petulance. 'I mean I did Julian Jarr last month, didenI, and it was fucking ruined by the same thing!'

'Nouveau Acid Rock,' Colin sniffed.

'*Ruined* by the – I mean, he was only talking about his drug bust, very personal stuff – '

'Public knowledge.'

' – and this dick-head of a lenser was only half-way up his nostril, wasn't he?'

'So?' Colin said again, maddeningly.

'So it's a one-to-one!' Mark yelled, losing advantage by too obvious a rage.

Reawakened by the shout, Kingsley looked across at them, momentarily puzzled, then raised the bottle.

'Cheers,' he said.

The two young men, eyes on each other, responded mechanically, the one not letting go of a triumphant gleam and the other not softening an affronted glare.

'He don't want it anyway,' Mark scowled.

'Who don't?'

'He don't,' said Mark, at last able to smirk a victory.

They turned from each other at the same time to look at Kingsley. Their sudden, and combined, attention disconcerted him, so that the whisky burnt his throat.

'Cheers,' he gasped, showing them the diminished bottle.

'Where's your plugs, then, pop?' Colin asked, without ceremony. 'I'll be needing more light than this, won't I?'

We all do, you little oik, thought the old man, with a sting at the back of his mouth, and a nod towards the dying Goethe.

15

A big silver moon shone down upon the crisply starched white
overlay of his narrow bed, and he heard a nightingale approach
and recede in the sloping, mimosa-clad wilderness of the
thirsty gardens below his window. He sat stiffly upright on a
rush chair late into the purple of the night, smoking and
sighing, imagining himself to be brave Aucassin looking for his
Nicolette in the Provençal romance, and then, after a while,
barely aware of the transition, he thought himself Nicolette
waiting in a cloth of silk for her Aucassin. Kingsley was not sure
which one to be, though he was capable of being neither. In his
life, back then, in his work, as ever, he also did not know
whether to search or whether to wait.

He had stayed on the top floor of an old stone house on the
edge of a steep village between Nice and Cap d'Ail for three out
of the four summers which preceded what he still called the
second German war. His landlady had been a white Russian
with a wall-eye, but it seemed to him, looking back, that
everything else in the place had been in harmonious balance.

About a third of the way into *Sugar Bush*, in chapters written
when there was a lace of ice in chill patterns upon his tall and
ill-fitting windows, Kingsley had taken Blackeyes (like Jessica
before her) on a working trip to the same magical coast. The sun
was burnishing the sea, the pine trees danced upon the land,
and nostalgia stung at his soul, like blood returning to frozen
hands and feet.

He had been fawningly timid, and much troubled by his
sexuality, in those years, when he had been in his twenties. But
the impotence and doubt were forgotten when he sat down like
Rumpelstiltskin in the wintry attic to spin Jessica's straw into
gold. By now, many months in, it at last seemed true that
he was going to produce another novel. Herb scents from

remembered hillsides wafted across his pages, but they were made by Jessica's perfumes. Kingsley had not travelled for almost a quarter of a century, and he had no idea that the past was not another country, or that his golden coast had since been swamped by vulgarities without number.

Jessica described to him the hotel where she and several other models had been photographed in someone's summer collection. Sulky postures in outlandish outfits, on a wide stone terrace where brightly coloured parasols flapped slightly in a honeyed breeze. He claimed he knew the place.

Height: Five feet six inches. Bust: Thirty-four. Waist: Twenty-two. Hips: Thirty-four. Shoe: Four, English. Glove: Six and a half, English. Hair: Black. Eyes: Dark Brown.

Eyes, black.

Blackeyes was half-way up to her knees in the sun-glitter of the sea, in Cannes, at Festival time. Her long black hair was loose, and she was 'topless'. Posing, turning, splashing up scoops of water, for a jostling horde of multilingual photographers, who instruct and plead, command and solicit.

Blackeyes, on the covers of a dozen magazines in four different languages, half-way up to her knees in the sea. A face and a figure for mass distribution, masturbation.

But did he ever show her in any ordinary conversation? Did she ever look at the sky, or eat a boiled egg, or remember her so recent childhood? Did she know that apes at sunset show signs of melancholy and agitation: and if she had been told this, would she have been interested? And did he allow her to sit on a rush chair, imagining herself to be a Nicolette walled up in a blank tower without a door, waiting for an Aucassin, hoping for release?

Jessica asked some or all of these questions, and a bait-bag full of more, as her eyes burnt up the pages. There were paragraphs where she could catch sight of the sea glittering through the pine branches, smell the basil, hear voices murmuring above the chink of tall glasses, but it was all just a backdrop to what she now knew to be a vast reservoir of grief.

At what point, she wondered, had she sashayed across the

line between using her body for these clothes, that product, this PR adjunct, and letting her soul itself become an object of trade? And how was she to reclaim herself, taking back what could be hers alone? Surely, not by words, merely words. She had to do something more dramatic than submit to the old man's text, even if *Sugar Bush* were little more (she considered) than dated literary adumbrations of her own experiences. There had to be a way out of the tower!

She looked over the side. It was too far to jump.

Down below, in the steep and closed-off streets of the principality, cars were howling and snarling in competition, sweeping past the enormous palace of an hotel. *Boring, boring, boring,* thought Blackeyes, on the private terrace, drinking champagne and nibbling at small, complicated messes on silver trays. None of the group seemed to be watching with genuine enthusiasm.

'There is speed. There *must* be skill. There is unquestionably a great deal of danger,' the bald host was saying, stretched on a lounger. 'So why, in heaven's name, is it quite so tedious?'

His name, if she could remember it aright, was Sebastian something or other. He sounded English except for the fact you could hear the commas in his speech.

'It is better when it is in the rain. More skid!' said Carlo, a young Italian, using the side of his hand to plane through the air in demonstration.

'Maybe we could do something about that,' an American joked. 'Throw some champagne over the balcony.'

'Mineral water, *if* you don't mind,' Sebastian said.

'Well, *I* think it's fascinating,' fluted in an Englishman of a kind now only to be found sponging in other climes. 'Even though I can't really tell which car is which, or who is in front, or who is out of it.'

Someone said he thought it was a Brazilian in the lead, and yawned.

'No, no,' Carlo objected. 'Is Italian. That's for sure.'

A few desultory laughs. A smell of burnt rubber in the air. Bubbles flowing in the scatter of bottles. A fugitive glance of light from the thin anklet on one of the long slender legs of the many long slender legs: two of the models who had shared the summer-collection assignment with Blackeyes, and three girls from Paris who seemed to be *filles de joie*.

Kingsley had taken these details from an exclamatory letter of Jessica's, full of dashes, hasty punctuations, and underlinings. She had sent it in response to his whining complaint about 'lack of colour', and even, as she held back her dismissive snort, an absence of 'glamour'.

'My dear girl,' he said, 'I've lived by far the greater part of my adult life in this street. I've seen countless numbers of these girls tip-tap-tuppettying along with those funny little cases they carry. They may very well be silly empty-heads, and I'll wager their private lives are as joyless and sordid as – as – well, never mind what as. Expense of spirit is a waste of shame, sort of thing. But, my dear girl, you're not a man, now are you? You don't seem to realize how inaccessible, how magical, how *glamorous* they can seem. No use you turning your nose up. It's not a word *I* propose to use. I'd sooner be seen dead! It's the concept, the ache of it, y'see. That's what I want. That's what you're not giving me. I shall have to pack it in, Jessie.'

Give me the dirt, is what he meant. She suspected that he wanted to excite himself, in the septuagenarian equivalent of an erection. Old men do not forget, they fumble. And grope.

But he had taken her dashes and exclamation marks as signals sent back from hell. The half-remembered fragments of banal conversation were fanned out like ostrich feathers made into pathetic adornment for the already damned. A gritty wind came up from the tilting, snarling streets below, and entered every orifice. Waiters appeared from time to time in white gloves, bearing food and drink that they would not allow their bare hands to touch for fear of sulphurous contamination. Later, too, he had one of the cars skid off the road in an accelerating scream.

Jessica was reluctant to concede that she might have underestimated him.

'I'm glad we are amused,' bald, ageing Sebastian had said,

heavily sarcastic. 'I'm delighted we are all enjoying ourselves so much.'

It was his party, and a hideously expensive one, so he insisted upon directing the tatters of conversation. After a while, bored by the cars, Sebastian began to philosophize. He told the story of 'one of those Northern gods', whose name temporarily eluded him, who pleaded with one of the mighty and malignant trolls to tell him the Secret.

'What secret?' asked the girl with the anklet.

'Shut up,' he said. 'Just shut up.'

Whatever the Secret was, it would be, what was the word?, vouchsafed to the petitioner if he gave up one of his eyes.

'Thor,' he said suddenly. 'It was Thor.'

'Well, he would be, wouldn't he? If he lost an eye,' the Englishman said, then whinnied.

Sebastian looked across the terrace at him, expressionless.

'Sore,' explained the interrupter, the whinny spent.

'I think,' said Sebastian, each word like a slap, 'that that is without any question the absolutely worst pun I've ever – '

'Sorry! Couldn't resist. Just slipped out. As the bishop said to – '

'No!' Sebastian shouted.

His face blanched under the tan, and his eyes had a crow's dull glare. Everyone felt uncomfortable. Mine Host looked too much like a psychotic monk, a Riviera Rasputin.

'Top up my glass, will you, darling?' he said to one of the girls.

When she had done so, Sebastian patted her thigh and smiled all around, absolving everyone.

'*Anyway*,' he said again. 'Pppsonk! Out comes the eye, torn out, in exchange for the Secret. So – now, tell me the Secret. Certainly, says the troll. The Secret is, watch with both eyes.'

The laughter which followed was in almost each case too obviously forced, although one of the two young Americans appeared to be genuinely amused. Such a contract, he said, reminded him of a turn-around clause – whatever that was - in a movie deal. Below them, the cars continued to howl, in meaningless sequence, and the conversation moved on to the coyote ethics of tinsel town and someone's claim that there were rats in the Hollywood palm trees.

Blackeyes took the chance, as the subject of money quickened the interest, to edge away from the terrace and go through the already wide open, mostly glass doors into the dusty pink caverns of the large suite beyond.

'My bank talks to me like that,' a voice was saying, in a mock rueful reference back to the Thor story, as she slipped away as unobtrusively as she could. A scatter of bored laughter stayed behind on the terrace, one of the worst human sounds.

She went on through a big, chandeliered room, where a soft rosewood glow reflected back on itself in oval mirrors speckled with age, to one of the several bedrooms that led off it by means of melancholy lobbies of marble. Here, she kicked off her shoes, stretched herself out on her back on top of the bed, and stared up at the creamily encrusted ceiling rose.

Blackeyes was tired: but she did not know what of.

(Maurice James Kingsley would never have let such an inelegant construction pass from his hand. The surmise must come from Jessica, as well as the way of expressing it. She is therefore talking about herself, or, rather, herself as by proxy she was at that time.)

Waste spelt itself out in her head. *Waste, waste* drummed her pulse. *Waste*, said the ceiling rose, in a whirl and a whorl.

'The silky folds of the curtains momentarily flowed outwards then sucked themselves back towards the window with a reluctant sigh. A door within the suite had opened and shut, with a soft thud. Her eyelids drooped, and the long black lashes made a lattice of dreamy haze, so that the heavy furniture took slow flight. The diminished buzz of the distant cars entered her drowsing mind as the summer murmur of bees going from flower to flower,' Kingsley's version said.

'What is the matter?' asked an Italian voice, with the hint of an intruding indefinite article. 'You are fatigued?'

She opened her eyes, but looked only at the ornamental rose above her, and did not answer.

84

Carlo smiled down at her. He sat on the bed, and took hold of her hand.

'You no like the cars?'

'No.'

'No?'

He began to stroke her arm, smiling at her. She did not turn her head.

'I think we are all tired,' he said.

'Yes.'

Carlo continued to stroke her arm with the tips of his fingers. Her hand stayed flat on the overlay. Her eyes stayed expressionless on the ceiling rose. In the next room, the chandelier tinkled in a minuscule quiver, catching a shifting current of air from the terrace in its luminous, crystal tentacles, and stifling it.

'You are beautiful,' he whispered, after a while.

'No,' she said.

'*Pretty* women think always they are beautiful. Why do *beautiful* women never think they are?'

She seemd to pull, to force, her attention from the ceiling, and compel her eyes to settle upon his lean and intent face. But she did not answer, and he did not stop his gentle stroking.

'Why?' he asked again, as though he really wanted to know. 'Why is that?'

'I'm tired,' she said.

Carlo smiled. His fingers moved less lightly, and began to dig into the softly rounded flesh of her upper arm. Blackeyes let her eyes go back to the ceiling rose.

'It is because when she come into the room all the eyes look on her. It is because when she walk, when she sit down, when she talk, when she do not talk, all the people look for the bad thing in her, the how you say? How you say? The flaw.'

The Flaw. Yes. She did not say it out loud.

He pulled his legs up on to the bed, and lay down beside her, without fuss, his head an inch or two from hers. They remained side by side for a whole minute, each looking up at the ceiling.

'What is up there?' he asked, eventually. 'What you see?'

'The ceiling.'

Her response was the kind of one she might have been expected to give to a stage hypnotist, Kingsley had said, drawing upon his own memories of just such a performance by a lithe, black-haired girl to a white-faced, evening-dressed Svengali at the old Chiswick Empire. The streets had had a blue glitter of rain under the street lamps when he left the variety theatre, and he had walked with his collar turned up, and an unidentifiable yearning gnawing inside him.

Kingsley had not assuaged that yearning by becoming Carlo for a paragraph or two, and what he wrote came mostly from Jessica, told to him over a cream tea in a warm hotel lounge in the depths of winter.

'You could rather too quickly find yourself behaving as though your body had values and demands quite other than who you were or who you *thought* you were,' she had said.

That's piffle, he thought, licking a sludge of cream from his top lip. What you mean is, you let yourself be rogered by any Johnny who cared to ask.

'Why are you looking at me like that, Jessica?'

'No reason.'

'Man overboard. Have I?' he asked, imagining there to be cream on his lip, and unaware that he had leaked his thoughts into a comprehensible mutter.

How you say, the flaw.

Carlo turned his body a little and began to stroke her face with the tips of just two fingers. She closed her eyes.

'But you have no flaw. Not you. Oh, no, no, no,' he purred, and she could feel his breath on her cheek. 'Your skin. Your bone. Your face. Perfect. Your body. Perfect. Perfect.'

His hand went down to her breast, lingered, then continued to her thigh, and back to the small swell of her belly. She lay still, her lips slightly parted, her breathing a little deeper, her eyes opening again.

Carlo released one of her breasts, licked at it, spoke in Italian, then pushed her legs apart.

'No,' she said, as though answering an ordinary question in a tepid conversation.

'Si!'

He clambered on top of her, with the awkward flail of too sudden an appetite, and his mouth slid around her face then clamped in half a bite half a suck on the fullness of her lips.

Suddenly, she came to life.

'No – No!' she forced her mouth free. 'Stop! No!'

He tried to grip her thrashing arms, astounded by the change.

'Hey – Hey – what is it – !'

'I don't-want-it – ' she hissed, twisting under him. 'No!'

But Carlo had got a firm hold on her wrists. He dragged her arms upwards, and pinioned them to the bed. He was extremely indignant.

'What you mean? What you mean? Who you think you are?'

'I mean No,' she said, kicking up with her legs, then arching her body in an attempt to get free. But he gripped harder, and pressed himself heavily down upon her.

'Bastard!' she hissed. 'Get off! Get off me! You filthy shit!'

Carlo was too busy and had too little breath to reply in kind. He had managed to open up her clothes, and was using the weight of his body and the urgency of his erection to man-oeuvre himself into a position where he could begin to thrust. Her struggles and thrashings seemed to be of no avail, and she let out a long scream of rage and hatred.

Out on the terrace, another and louder cry from Blackeyes made the girls exchange questioning glances, and stir a little. The men pretended not to notice, but their expressions changed. One of the Americans put his glass down on the stone balustrade, with too firm a clunk.

The noise from within the suite did not stop, and could not for long be ignored.

Sebastian rose with pretended heaviness from his lounger.

'Really,' he said, with would-be insouciance. 'This place gets more like the centre court at Wimbledon every day. Bad-mannered, indisputably suburban, and crowded with shrieking females.'

There were a few laughs as he ambled towards the suite. The

boredom was lifting. The guests looked at each other, put down their drinks, and followed.

Blackeyes, given strength by her fury, and more animated than anyone had ever before seen her, had thrown off the Italian. He bumped down into the shaggy white pile beside the bed, and she scrambled past him towards the door, in much disarray. Carlo got to his feet in such a swift, grabbing lurch that he was able to get between her and the door.

When Sebastian tapped on the door with a satiric politeness and opened it, Blackeyes had her back to the wall, face contorted, and fingernails clawing out at the Italian as he came at her again.

'What the hell is going on?' Sebastian asked, without obvious anger.

Carlo let go of her. He backed off a little, spreading his hands in resigned indignation.

'She go mad. Crazy,' he said.

Blackeyes lowered her hands, and looked at Sebastian, the fire dying out in her eyes. Her dress was torn open at the front, and her mostly exposed breasts rose and fell as she continued to pant.

'I had hoped this was some sort of game. I hoped that what I was seeing was not what it looked like,' Sebastian said. 'This is intolerable. Intolerable! Do I have to remind you that you are my guest!'

Blackeyes stared back at him, puzzled. The bald man with the little round belly that wobbled over his reptile-skin belt was addressing *her*.

'Me?' she asked. 'You're talking to me?'

'You!' he bellowed. 'Yes, you!'

Some of the others were pressing together in the doorway behind him, like spectators at a road accident. They had odd smiles on their faces, probably of embarrassment.

Sebastian went up to her, anger giving place to the avuncular, and, although she stiffened against the wall, he put his hand on her shoulder.

'Blackeyes. My darling. You must now allow yourself to get

into this sort of state. It is without dignity, let alone grace. Can't you see that?'

She stared at him, a nerve fluttering in her throat. She looked across at the others, peering in at her. She moved her eyes to take in Carlo, who gave her a lopsided smile and gestured with his hands again.

'This is a *party*,' said Sebastian. 'Now, isn't it?'

'But – ' she said, out of a closed throat.

'So what exactly is the problem here?'

'But – ' she said. 'But I am not a – '

She stopped. Again, she stared at him. Again, she looked across at the others, still silent and half-smiling at the open door.

'You're not a what, darling? Not a sensible girl, mmm?'

His hand squeezed her shoulder, in a vaguely threatening grip.

'I am not a prostitute,' she said, with precision.

At the door and in the room, from everybody, there was a moment of watchful silence. It was as though, in the very careful enunciation of the sentence, a code had been broken.

Blackeyes looked again from face to face, and then she began to laugh. The tension went out of her body. Her laugh grew and grew, but she did not put a hand up to her face. Sebastian watched, waited, then smiled, then also started to laugh. Carlo threw his head back, chopped the air with his hands, and roared. The men and the young women pressing at the doorway laughed.

Eventually, someone went back out to the terrace and brought in a few of the bottles and glasses. Blackeyes cried a little into the cup of her hand, then laughed some more. The bubbles climbed in joyous columns in the crystal flutes. The light went slowly purple in the sky, and the chandeliers blazed brighter and brighter by the moment.

In time, the willowy Parisienne with the thin ankle-chain of gold helped Blackeyes out of her torn clothing, and then both of them lay down on the same bed under the same ceiling rose on either side of Carlo, who retained the same name and the same ejaculatory cry of repeated triumph both in the tender deceits of the fiction and the savage accuracies of Jessica's recollection.

16

What a day!

Uncle Maurice in a clean shirt and a new bow tie had brought along a little boat with a stiff white sail, and they had floated it on the Round Pond in Kensington Gardens. This had been early in the morning, although Jessica had always remembered it as much later in the day, when the light had begun to fade.

They had eaten hamburgers in gluggy pools of tomato sauce, and knickerbocker glories with long thin spoons at lunchtime in the high street down from the park. Afterwards, they walked hand in hand along wide pavements, whistling for a taxi. The one they found took them all the way across the river to the fun-fair, where she sat on wooden horses that went round and round, up and down, up and down. And then another big black taxi all the way back to the curve of Regent Street before the shops closed, where the best thing of the best day had happened.

It was late enough for a little girl, and a long way home.

She fell asleep in the car, holding the new doll Clementine tightly in her arms. The darkening road unwound itself deeper into the shires, escaping the long fingers and dirty nails of the city. Hedges thick with summer, and dry stone walls began to narrow the route. Flat seas of orange and red, low on the horizon but as wide as the sky, began to blacken at the top, break up, drift apart.

'Well, now. That *was* a busy old day, wasn't it?' Uncle Maurice said, as though he had trouble making conversation, and after he had said nothing for many miles.

He looked sidelong, with a determined twinkle, not realizing that his niece had gone to sleep. Kingsley considered waking her with one of his merry quips, but stopped what he had been about to invent. Let the sweet little thing slumber.

'Jessica,' he said instead, but not for her to hear.

He put his attention back to the road. There was a slow and very agricultural lorry in front, labouring through the gears as the road climbed steeply and skewered to the left between lines of beeches.

What a nuisance this lorry was becoming. It was tall, filthy, and slatted: he thought he could see the dark shapes of farm animals between the slats, and this disturbed him. The road had dwindled too much, and was winding too unpredictably, to allow him to pass safely, even though it was almost dark now, and any oncoming vehicles would splash out swaths of light.

Kingsley had not easily learnt how to drive, and had four times failed his test, once for abusing the examiner. He had a poor sense of speed and distance, or the ratio of the two, and panicked easily. In less than a year from this day he was to give up driving altogether, partly on the advice of a drunken fool of a magistrate: an occasion for an Occasional Piece denouncing both the internal combustion engine and the petty tyrannies of badly administered law.

Christ Jesu On High, he thought, I hate this light. I loathe and detest the countryside.

'The da-ay Thou ga-a-vest Lord is o-o-ver – ' sang the gloomiest part of his mind, charioting him back to the fucking school fucking chapel . . .

Kingsley slowed still more, letting the belching lorry crawl a greater distance ahead of him. There was a creeping tingle of pain in his chest, a dull ache at the back of his eyes, and a whiteness at his knuckles. He was holding the steering wheel too tightly, and he was holding his teeth together too tightly.

Furthermore, he wanted a pee.

Tension and distress were coming towards him from the bumpy dark fields. The hunching, overladen trees at the edge of the road were too busy nodding and whispering to themselves to keep these visitors at bay in the open land where they belonged.

An old wooden signpost, unaffected by more recent depredations and the latest Ministry regulations, lurched crookedly into view in the headlight dazzle. The Angells, it said: meaning, less ethereally, Great Angell and Little Angell, adjoining hamlets in half-forgotten dells that shared a bell-less Norman church and an abandoned primary school.

Kingsley looked in his rear-view mirror, which was an act he rarely bothered to do when driving. The road behind him was dark and empty.

He swung the car off the A-road, and on to the near-track signposted with such celestial promise. The lorry with the load of beasts chugged onwards, up and then over the brow of the hill.

The car came to a halt on a grass verge wider than the minor road itself. Kingsley pulled the handbrake on, and it made a metallic groan of a noise. He thought it would wake up the little girl, but she did not stir.

He kept his hands on the steering wheel, knuckles still showing white, and stared straight ahead through the windscreen, which was smeared with crushed insects. The filth of summer.

'Who's a sleepyhead?' he said to her, without turning.

Kingsley sat with his hands tight on the wheel for what felt like the eternity of torment promised to the damned. He watched the last of the light die on the topmost branches of a straggle of trees on the brow of the grassy knoll to his right. Some late crows flapped slow and black to the same trees, and he followed their flight with a bitter squint of attention which could have suggested that they were bearing bits of himself away to their wretched roost.

He switched off his lights, and looked for the moon.

'I will have a pee,' he said to himself, with a steady precision. 'I will get out of the car, walk a few yards behind it, and piss on a buttercup or a daisy.'

What is it? said an older, deeper part of his head, at the same time. What dreadful thing is it that has happened?

He was no more adept than most people sensibly choose to be at recognizing the failure of what had once been the most personal, the most tender, and the most valiant of hopes. But now, this evening, in this wayside interval immeasurable by the clock, Kingsley had not even the flimsiest of defences when the realization flew in at him beak and claw out of the low sky.

The calamitous truth which he had not been able to acknowledge until this moment of the deepest misery, hands on the wheel, was that he would never be able to fulfil the high promise he did not even know he had made to himself. Maurice James Kingsley, lying in the cropped grass on the far side of the cricket pavilion at school, had settled upon the vocation of literature: a vocation, properly so called, which had to be approached with at least as much fear, awe and reverence as that necessary for the priesthood. If he were to serve it, then assuredly the scourges of self-discipline and the rigours of faith that would have to be called forth from him, bent as though in prayer over the page, demanded nothing less than the total commitment of his being: a commitment which took its measure only from his abilities, the equivalent of grace. Talent, in other words. Talent, the old coinage. And if the talent fell short, then everything else about the calling, the commitment, was nothing but an empty and posturing impertinence.

Sitting there in the fast approaching darkness, the sleeping child next to him, Kingsley saw the enormity of his adolescent vows for the first time since he had made them.

He saw that the novel he had so recently finished, his third, was banal and dishonest, even though it had been praised to low heavens by those who read it. Worse still, the book had been preceded by two others which were no less meretricious. Oh, woe: then woe: and then more woe. And each inner cry without a trace of irony, that normal compensation for the defeated, the disappointed and the self-deceiving.

Kingsley did not know why this cruel revelation had settled upon him with such complete certainty at this particular moment. It was not a passing depression, nor a fleeting illusion made out of the tiring activities of the day. The seeping away of the light had nothing to do with it, nor did the melancholy distances of the moon as it rode through archipelagos of cloud, so heavily trailed with literary associations, temporarily corrupt his mind. A lorry full of trapped animals could not explain the devastation, any more than the presence of the sleeping child and the china doll she clutched in her arms.

Any more than the sleeping child and the china doll she clutched in her arms.

Kingsley's wriggling thoughts at last buckled in on themselves, and choked him.

Any more than the sleeping child and —

Kingsley jerked forward, with a twist of the mouth, and suddenly clicked open the car door. He almost ran from the vehicle, towards the rear, until a spurt of nausea hurtling up his dried throat made him stop and bend and retch.

When he straightened, Kingsley walked on across a soft tufty carpet spangled with as many tiny gleams of star as there were in the summer sky above him, and saw the progenitor of all the dark, amorphous forms he was to see so many more times in all the years that lay ahead of him.

'A pee,' he said to himself, in what would have been a sob if he had spoken aloud. 'I – badly – want – a – pee.'

He unbuttoned his flies, and forked out his cock with thumb and forefinger. It had been his secret habit since he had been about ten years old to hum, in his head, 'On The Sunny Side Of The Street' when urinating. Once again, here in the grass, he tried to remind himself not to forget his hat and coat, but the tuneful admonition would not come.

'Who's a sleepyhead?' he whispered as the orange bow arched out from him in a steamy splatter.

> O My Darling, O My Darling
> O My Darling Clementine
> You are gone and lost forever
> Lost forever, Clementine

The moon sailed overhead, silver lady of the night, and the stars wheeled slow and unnoticed in the rural sky as Maurice James Kingsley completed the splashing of the buttercups and daisies and walked back to the car, without doing up his flies.

17

Trundle, trundle, and out came the stone cold body of the beautiful young woman. Jamieson pulled in as many of his muscles as he could. His eyes rolled for a moment, and then steadied. His tongue stuck against the roof of his mouth, and felt as though it were twice its normal size.

'Yes. I'm sorry, Mr Jamieson,' said Blake. 'It's never a pleasant job, this.'

'I'm afraid I have a very weak stomach,' the swollen tongue managed. 'I – I'd really rather not – ah – '

He stared down at the dead woman.

'Take your time, sir.'

'I – no. I don't think I – '

'Take your time.'

Jamieson suddenly lost control of his face. He whirled away, and, with an odd delicacy, just managed to catch the sudden spurt of his bile with his raised and cupped hands.

'Oh! I'm so – ' he tried to apologize, deeply shamed, but his throat closed, stifling the words.

The Detective Inspector handed him a large white handkerchief, silently, not looking in the least solicitous. Jamieson wiped his stickied hands, for the slimy bile had made a sort of web between his fingers. He tried to straighten his shoulders while doing this, as though to reaffirm a minimal dignity.

'Don't think I shall be having my usual lunch today,' he said, out of the same impulse.

But then he almost vomited again, swallowed down the spasm, and, all defences shattered, smiled plaintively at the policeman. Blake's face made no returning concession.

'Can you give me any help? Do you recognize her? Do you know her?'

Jamieson, churning inside, and conscious of the poor

impression he had made as a man among men, looked around the white, half-tiled walls as though seeking another means of escape. Each ceramic oblong stayed in place. The walls did not move.

'I really don't see why *I* should be involved in – '

'But *do* you know her?' Blake cut in.

Jamieson hesitated, and half-looked at the body again. His fingers tightened around the now soiled handkerchief, and he dabbed it to his lips.

'I've only once before ever seen a – someone's who's dead – it's very difficult, almost impossible for me to – '

'She knew you,' Blake said, once again slicing into the havers.

Jamieson held himself very still, and affected to look puzzled.

'Oh? How do you know that? Who says so?'

'Her note says so.'

'What note?'

'A note found on her body.'

Who are these other people standing around? thought Jamieson. Why do some of them have ballpens and notebooks?

'I don't have orgasms,' said a flat voice in his head. The dangerous, wicked little bitch! Fancy being so bloody ungrateful!

But did a man think like this . . .?

Kingsley's narrative had ended with the water smoothing itself out over the black hair of the girl, a bathetic conclusion which left everything else in the hands of the police and the coroner's court. The scenes involving Detective Inspector Blake were additions to *Sugar Bush*, and showed a cruder imagination at work. They were like a ramshackle annexe built on to the side of a small Georgian house, an extension that destroyed the proportions and questioned the value of the main building. Hammer and nails and hardboard brought to the now muddied-up site by Jessica.

Yes! Bang, bang, bang. *Yes! He did think like this!* Thud, thud thud.

A note? *A note?* Oh, my Christ.

'Didn't you tell me she was – um – naked when they – I mean, you said she didn't have any clothes – ' Jamieson said, almost managing not to stutter.

'A note found *in* her body, sir.'

Jamieson stared at Blake, affronted. He frowned and cleared his throat, then tried a smile.

'I'm not altogether sure I understand what you are saying – ' He stopped.

'Me?' he said again, suddenly. 'She mentions *me*? How? I mean, in what way?'

Blake measured his man.

'Offensively, sir.'

Jamieson's eyes blazed for the briefest moment in what would have been, for him, a routine exertion of power, and, in this case, social superiority: but he was too shaken to play the familiar old game. Instead, he went to wipe his damp face with the handkerchief he still clutched, and then saw the sticky strands of his own bile clinging to it.

'Here,' he said gruffly, holding it out to Blake.

'So that is why we asked you to try and make a positive identification, and give us any other help you can,' Blake said, ignoring the proffered handkerchief.

Jamieson looked at the stained linen in his hand, feeling foolish.

'I'll get this laundered, of course,' he said, putting it into his trouser pocket.

'Would you like to take another look at her? To make sure?'

'No!' Jamieson spun away, too violently, and his voice too shrill.

'I think perhaps – yes,' he began again, when nobody else spoke. 'She's very like a girl who was used a few times by my company. I mean, I'm sure she is.'

'Used, sir?'

'For modelling. In advertisements, and – She's a model.'

'Her name?'

'I don't know her real name. Only the one she used professionally. Blackeyes.'

'Blackeyes?'

'Bloody silly, eh?' Jamieson said, with a man-to-man smile.

'Thank you, sir. That is very useful.'

'Does she mention any other – um – names?'

'What?'

'I mean, in her suicide note.'

'I didn't say anything about suicide, sir.'

Jamieson gaped. He could see, as he recovered, the hardness of the policeman's expression, and its complete lack of amiability.

'What we always say in the Force, and it seems to be true,' said Blake, staring at him, 'is that people who deliberately drown themselves don't often go to the trouble of taking all their clothes off, sir. In fact, if you'll pardon my smile, they sometimes dress their bloody selves up, sir, in order to do it in what they think is style, sir.'

Pardon your smile? thought Jamieson. What smile?

'Do they?' he asked, feeling more and more nervous.

'And there's another thing, sir.'

Blake deliberately waited, and Jamieson was compelled to ask what it was.

'Her fingernails, sir. They were all broken, and her fingers themselves are what you would call damaged, sir. Here. Look at this.'

Blake pointed to the dead hands, and then folded his arms, waiting once again, but Jamieson said nothing.

'What do you think, sir? Looked as though she might have been trapped somewhere, don't it? Tried to claw her way out, mm? But that's just a guess, at this stage. Perhaps it's just my imagination. You know – lovely lady, trapped, all that sort of stuff.'

'Why are you looking at me like this? You surely don't think – '

'Like what, sir?'

'Now look here, officer – !'

'Look here what, sir?'

Jamieson went as red as Jessica intended, but none of his urbanity or his bluster was of any use to him in this dreadful room that stank of a long forgotten biology laboratory. The torn hands he had looked at were hands that had held and stroked his rearing penis. The pale, full mouth he had seen had enclosed it and stroked it, too. The inconsiderate slut.

'When did your company last employ her, sir? And for what? And where?'

And he knew there would be so many more such questions, coming in a tumble one after the other, with a snap of the eyes or the neck, all leading up to the inevitable crudity, which would not be expressed in precisely the basic terms each man had already put to himself.

'And when did you last fuck her, sir?'

18

Savage rocks unsoftened by any wisp of vegetation stretched, climbed and fell and rose again as far as the hot, gritty and tired eye could see. The sun beat down in a furnace of open sky as though it were envenomed, determined to torment any living thing which dared to crawl or slither or simply lie there panting beneath its rays. Even the brooding locals slouched slowly about with the grubby hoods of their burnouses dragged up over their heads. They stared back with a dull black glitter at any sweating European who had so forgotten history as to clap his hands and ask for something.

Blackeyes, who was wearing little, had two men holding umbrellas to protect her from the intimidating dazzle. The donkey which waited with a bowed head had a straw hat, through which its ears poked, but seemed to be in distress, and not just from the relentless black flies.

The Atlas Mountains appealed to the director's sense of magnitude. He consistently behaved towards his crew and his assorted writers as though he had the whole world on his shoulders.

'You'll come down this track,' he was explaining to Blackeyes. 'And when you reach that funny-looking boulder there, you see it? The one which looks like a Hovis loaf. When you get there you'll get a signal. You rein in this stupid fucking animal, and then you reach back behind you and *Blackeyes*. Are you listening to me?'

'Who are those people?' she asked.

'What people?'

'Those. Up there.'

She pointed a long bare arm at a ridge above them. A group of North Africans were strung out in a straggling line across it, looking down upon the crew, evoking childhood memories in several of those present of Red Indians making a sudden appearance (with a beat of drums) in a Western.

Arnie the director was not making such a film.

'Jack!' he bellowed to a small round man with continents of sweat mapped on his vest. 'Who are all those? Up there!'

Jack gave them a quick look, but he already knew.

'Berbers,' he shouted back. 'That's what they are.'

Arnie was irritated. They might interfere with his shot. They might even be, well, dangerous. He looked around for someone to blame.

One of the men holding an umbrella over Blackeyes said that they were no trouble, so long as you took not a blind bit of notice of them.

'Years ago the second unit for wasname was here, the Lawrence thing. They used a lot of them,' he explained. 'What they got was lunch. Every day they got some grub. There's a lot of hungry whatyoucallits in these bleed'n hills. Nomads. I expect they're looking for the same from us. Anything'll do, except pork.'

Arnie was incredulous. He stared up at the ridge, and then back at the man with the umbrella, suddenly indignant.

'You mean they're waiting for our catering truck?'

Jack had toiled up the baked track to come closer to what he called His Lord And Master. He had a manner of speaking which demeaned the director without actually straying into outright insolence.

'That's right, old son,' he said. 'Nosh.'

'Then tell them to fuck off!' Arnie flared.

He turned back to Blackeyes, who had not taken her eyes from the distant line of tribesmen.

'OK, darling. Get yourself into the cart. And when you stretch back, will you for God's sake remember to *smile* – '

'Those people,' she said, not looking at him, her eyes filling.

'Never mind them. They won't interfere with you. We'll shoo them away.'

'No – listen!' she said, suddenly animated. 'They are *hungry*.'

The director stared at her. Little round Jack stared at her. The

102

two men with the umbrellas, the make-up lady, and the props man stared at her, for Blackeyes had not so far made a single interjection out of turn, nor shown the slightest trace of any untoward emotion.

'Blackeyes,' said Arnie, warningly.

But a tear had splashed down her cheek. She was wearing blue mascara, so this was not thought to be a good idea.

'Blackeyes,' Arnie wagged a finger at her. 'I hope you're not going to be difficult.'

She made the mistake of putting a hand to her eyes, which were now welling freely with tears.

'No!' cried the make-up lady.

What could be the cause of this unprofessional display? Kingsley had asked, with what he imagined to be deceptive cunning: as though a brisk nudge in the ribs, sufficient to crack the bone, could properly be so called.

Blackeyes wept without restraint. Her sobs encompassed the dry rocks, the patient donkey, the sweating crew, the watching Berbers, the vast sky, the burning sun, all of which were being turned there and then into images on film: images of money, and of possession. The music would be added later.

'Jesus Christ,' said Arnie. 'There's nothing to cry about!'

Eventually, she stopped. They wiped her face, and reapplied the blue mascara, and touched up the other cosmetics on her face. She apologized, and got up into the cart, which was full of oranges and lemons, so globular and polished and vivid that it was unlikely they were real.

19

Four men sat in squeakily soft chairs of white leather leaning forward in a diminished light to watch flickering images seized from the heat of day in another continent. Luscious music licked the harsh peaks and bare rocks as though they were lollipops. An upward tilt carried the brass and the percussion to the huge sun burning a hole in the endless sky, releasing a tense little trill of violins as the rays momentarily scorched out all sense of shape. Tremendous, said the pictures: don't worry about it, said the music. Unobtainable: purchasable.

Out of the fierce orange glow, the rocks emerged again, a rough track winding through them. The music relaxed. A donkey came into sight, pulling a cart. On the cart was a lovely young woman, the reins loosely held in her long fingers. At a twist in the path, by an oddly shaped boulder, she passed her hand across her brow, looked up into the furnace of the heavens, smiled an enigmatic smile, and reached back into the open cart, which was full of the biggest oranges and lemons anyone ever did see. The stretch of her arm exposed half her breast.

Buried amongst the oranges and lemons was a little bottle, which she pulled out with a triumphant wink at the now acknowledged camera, accompanied by a crescendo from the hidden orchestra. She held out her prize, and tilted it to drink. A trio of voices sang to meet the sudden close-up of the bottle.

> When the lady wants it
> Clean and Fresh
> Wherever
> Whenever
> It's Orlo she goes for
> Orlo-o
> Orlo-o-o
> Orlo-o-o-o-o!

The images died and the music stopped.

Four men sat silent in their soft white cradles of leather, looking at the blank screen. Each one then shifted a little, making the smallest of squeaks.

'Mmm,' said the first man, *primus inter pares*.

'Yes,' said the second man. 'I rather tend to agree.'

'Mmmm,' repeated the first man.

'Something's not quite there, is it?' said the third man.

The fourth man, who was the youngest, stared at the floor and then stared at the wall.

The first man sighed a thoughtful and masterful sort of sigh.

'There's a sense in which, certainly, something is – missing,' the second man said, nodding as he spoke, and nodding after he had finished.

'Mmm?' said the first man, with the barest hint of a question.

'The whole point, of course, is the Wherever, Whenever,' said the youngest, defensively. He was the copywriter. 'It has to be seen in that context. Part of a series.'

'Mmm,' again, and an ambiguous squeak of white leather.

'The second one, if there is a second one I mean, has her ascending the Eiffel Tower with a pannier, and I hope the – '

'Good!'

Jeff, the copywriter, was startled by the abruptness of the transformation from the labial to the exclamation.

And so were the others:

'Yes,' said the second man, sitting up straighter. 'I tend to go along with that. Sophistication.'

'More – um – more – ' searched the third.

'I like those mountains,' the first man cut in before the word could be found. 'The Atlas Mountains, are they not? Is that where they went? Yes. I think you've got a handle upon a viable concept there, with ongoing sequentiality. Well done, Jeff.'

Jeff felt an obscure shame, like a flash of pain in some deep ganglion.

'I was trying for something out of the rut. Thank you,' he said, then looked at the floor again, and at the wall again, while the second man stared at his own knees and the third folded his arms in what those who knew him understood to be a gesture of anxiety.

'She's a ravishing young female,' Roberts chuckled. 'Sense of humour, too. After a fashion.'

'That's what I meant,' said the second man, in a too swift attempt at exculpation. 'I don't think that that necessarily comes across. Her humour.'

'What do you want her to do?' Roberts frowned. 'Laugh at the product?'

'No, of course not! I didn't mean that, William – '

'I wasn't talking about her as a model or whatever. The sense of humour I'm referring to comes out in her private life. She's very – laid back. No – what do they say nowadays?'

'Off the wall,' Jeff said, and they all laughed and squeaked.

A brief discussion followed on the vulnerability of English English to the onslaughts of its bigger and more vigorous linguistic neighbour. Kingsley invented this conversation specifically in order for him to introduce a few feline asides which did not belong to such characters in such a swill-bucket trade. A passage which was easy, predictable, and popular, for it discharged old prejudices under the guise of street-wise modernity.

Jessica, when reading it, was not concerned with what she thought of as Old Fart jokes about degrees of precedence or purity between different dialects. She puzzled, instead, about the man Roberts: and then realized that Kingsley had cloned him out of Jamieson. They were the same man in her memories. It was a complication which temporarily threatened her slowly burgeoning scheme, until she decided that Jamieson should be given two new middle names.

'William. You dog,' said the first man to Roberts (Jamieson), exaggerating the admiration because he felt he had not said the right things earlier.

Roberts, duly pleased, pretended not to know what the sycophant was talking about.

'Her *private* life, eh?'

'Oh. That. Yes,' Roberts chuckled. 'Well. I'll give you a little for-instance, shall I? All boys together, but no tales out of school, if you please.'

Jeff went to stand, but sat down again.

'No sooner had we perched ourselves on the bar stools, and before she'd even got her sweet little tongue into a bloody Pina Colada or whatever, she picks up a nut – you know, out of the dish on the bar – and looks straight at me, as solemn as a parson, and without batting an eye, do you know what she says? "I – don't have – orgasms." '

There was laughter, not wholly untroubled, which Jeff had difficulty in accepting. The grimace he made, however, was sufficiently close to the expressions on the other faces to pass without notice.

'And was she right?' asked the third man, on the slope of the sniggers.

Roberts simply raised one eyebrow, and two of them laughed again, heartily enough to make the chairs squeak in repeated sequence.

20

Blackeyes lay on the bed, one leg under the clothes, her hair loose on the blue silk of the pillows, the dark gleam in her eyes directed at Roberts, who was standing in front of a long mirror, putting on a striped tie.

'Rather odd of me, no doubt,' he was saying, like someone listening to himself, 'to tie my tie before I put on my trousers. But that's always been the way I've done it, y'see. Can't abide change.'

He was conformist in most of his social and political opinions, and had no religious ones: but he liked to think that he was regarded as something of an eccentric, in endearing little ways which tempered the enjoyment of conspicuous wealth and the exercise of power.

As he tightened the knot, he whistled under his breath.

'I would have liked to have hopped across to Paris. Do you like Paris?'

She moved a shoulder, and supposed so.

'Quite an *enthusiast*, aren't you?' he smiled, turning from the mirror to look at her. It was an irritated smile.

Blackeyes was not paying him attention because she could hear faint strains of dance music from somewhere below, in the hotel. A band was playing 'I'll See You In My Dreams', with a melancholy lilt made sadder by distance.

'Are you tired? Or bored, or something?'

'Yes,' she said.

He decided that she must mean she was tired, and hopped on one leg as he pulled on his trousers.

'Funny the way people dress themselves,' he said, wanting to talk, but still more to listen to what he had to say.

'Mm,' she said, trying hard to pick up the music.

'I suppose it's one of the first complicated things we learn. All the buttons and armholes and leg-holes. Whenever I dress, no matter what stage, somewhere in the back of my mind I always say to myself – well, at least you've got your left sock on, old chap. Or, at least you've done up four of your shirt buttons.'

He frowned at his own image, disturbed by something he had said, unaware that he had become, for the moment, a medium for conducting Kingsley's oldest anxiety, one already reported in these as yet unedited pages.

Blackeyes wanted him to finish putting his clothes on, stop talking and go out of the door. There was a remote tune reaching her mind, touching it, and she knew that it meant to say something, but the sense of its messages stayed out of understanding. The furniture in the room was also patterned in some configuration that tried to speak, but, again, the language remained muffled, untranslated.

Roberts turned from the long mirror once more, and stared at her.

'Exactly as though something utterly dreadful was going to happen before I finished dressing,' he said.

He sat on the edge of the bed and frowned down at his stockinged feet.

'God knows what, though.'

Out of nothing and out of nowhere, he felt, a drift of sadness had enveloped him. It was like standing in the smoke of an autumn bonfire. Weeds were burning.

'Are you not well? Is something wrong?' he asked, twisting his neck round so that he could turn his own incomprehensible change of mood into an accusation.

'No,' Blackeyes said. 'Nothing.'

He wriggled his toes in their socks, and wondered what was wrong. After all, it had been an exceptionally pleasurable hour or so, this bedroom joust. He had not managed to come twice in such a session for many years, but he had done so this evening. Was this the trouble?

'Good. That's a good girl,' he sighed, and looked around the floor for his shoes. Quick! Get them on! Exactly as though something dreadful were about to happen . . .

Blackeyes watched him put on his shoes. If I were a dog, she thought, I might think it was his feet he was putting on. She corrected 'dog' to 'bitch'. I'd sniff for all the smells. I'd . . . bite the hand that fed me!

'There's a band,' she said. 'I can hear a dance band.'

'Oh, they have these things here from time to time. This was a very swish hotel in the twenties and thirties, so I'm told. Before every Tom, Dick and Harry went abroad for their holidays.'

He stood up, and stamped his feet, not too hard.

'It's nice,' she said. 'It sounds nice. The music.'

She wasn't really talking to him. If I were a drawing, she thought, a woman on the bed in a strip cartoon (ah! strip!), I'd have a little balloon coming up out of my mouth, with 'It's nice. It sounds nice. The music.' written inside it.

'All these big palaces on the south coast, *cor ain't they grand*!' he went on, without a balloon. 'They're marooned in their own past, of course. That's why they have all these Fancy Dress things and whatnot. Nostalgia. Playing all the old numbers. I'd hate to go myself. Make me feel as though I was being pickled in embalming fluid. I've got better stuff than that in my old dick, eh?'

'No,' she said. 'It's nice. It sounds nice.'

'Oh, not for a modern girl like you, darling,' he laughed, beginning to cast off the threatening melancholy. He put his hand down to the front of his trousers, and patted himself with an almost ruefully proprietorial affection: the steed is back in the stable.

'We'll do this again soon, I very much hope,' he said as he bent to kiss her, unnecessarily flicking his tongue across her lips, gin and tonic still riding his breath. He knew where he could find her.

She watched the door close.

'Why not?' she said, and lay still, not considering things but counting them.

There were twelve, thirteen, fourteen metal links on the dangling chain beside the door. There were two, three chairs.

Four mirrors. Forty-seven, forty-eight, forty-nine folds in the velvety fall of the curtains at the curve of the window. Five seagulls in the picture on the far wall. Seven, eight, nine roses in the picture on the near wall.

How many black and brown hexagons in the rug on the fitted carpet?

One, two, three, four . . .

It was being alone in a room that could be the worst thing. The second, was being made to talk. The third, was having to talk to yourself, especially if by some mischance you found that you were listening.

. . . five, six, seven, eight, nine . . .

But when Jessica read this, she vehemently rejected it as a 'reason' for her own former, admitted promiscuity. She concluded that Kingsley had been writing about himself, mixing his own eccentricities into the girl's thoughts. A nasty image came walking towards her: the old man's grey-tufted head perched wrinkling and simpering on the young woman's slender body, a grotesque transplant.

Jessica shuddered inside, and looked down at her own limbs.

. . . ten, eleven, twelve, thirteen . . .

Blackeyes stopped counting things and shapes, and put on her clothes to go to the window.

Illuminated in the July night by floodlights in the shrubberies fronting it, the big hotel looked as white and sugary as a cake-shop confection, but this was not of course apparent from within its decorative crenellations and pepper-pot towers. The upper windows had views of the sea, darkly glinting at the moment under a summer moon.

At one of these, the curtains drawn back around her, Blackeyes stood, as still as though she were awaiting the first sighting of a particular ship: but it was the spilled sound of the visiting dance band she was attending to, and the cargo boat out on the sea, lights glowing fore and aft, was made by her into an embodiment of the melody she could hear from further below in the hotel.

Entered by a long half-glassed terrace of effulgent plants and white wrought-iron traceries, the ballroom glowed with the

111

adornments, the Cupids, and the pale plaster rose-petals of pre-war decades. The preposterous swank of one generation had become the fancy dress of another, so that what was once an assertion of wealth by means of confident pastiche was now a comical and yet faintly wistful vulgarity.

Tonight, a dance band which had made a moderate name for itself imitating arrangements from the swingtime days was bouncing out tunes that seemed to swell in grateful recognition of their surroundings. The trace of knowing derision which belongs to almost all mimicry had dissolved in the larger conceits of a probably long since dead interior designer. Even the principal singer found that the calculated smirk he normally needed beneath his severely parted, boot-black hair was no longer an appropriate irony.

He stepped forward, nodding to the beat, and began to sing 'The Clouds Will Soon Roll By', an optimistic lyric interestingly compromised by the plaintiveness of the tune.

Or so thought the copywriter Jeff, who liked to measure the relative values of cheap emotions. He had once seen an old woman in a greetings-card shop moving her lips as she read the verse in one birthday card after another, and he had realized for the first time that neither the ability nor the motives of those who had written the banal little rhymes were at issue: the old woman was seeking the most appropriate clutch of words to express the truth of *her* feelings for whoever she wanted to send the card to. She was the one who brought the truth, and the dignity, to what had been written without either.

> I hear a robin singing
> Upon a tree-top high
> To you and me he's singing
> The clouds will soon roll by –

The song passed through floors and windows to reach Black-eyes in her room. She could hear better now that her visitor had gone, for he had creaked the old floorboards and snuffled and huffled as well as interrupted with loud words.

'I can't stay here,' she thought, in a sudden uprush of anxiety.

112

'I have to get out of here.'

> Somewhere the sun is shining
> So honey don't you cry
> We'll find a silver lining
> The clouds will soon roll by.

Jeff put his glass down on a table near the doors, intending to leave. The ballroom was full of middle-aged dancers who swirled around the floor with a self-conscious or imitative grace. One of the ladies had a flower in her hair.

They are trying to hold something that has gone, he thought. They will wake later with bad dreams, and start to quarrel. The petals will fall to the floor, the flesh sag out of the corset.

> Each little fear and sorrow
> Only brings you closer to me
> Just wait until tomorrow
> What a happy day that will be.

The singer was opening his hands wider and wider, and the light gleamed on his slicked black hair. Jeff still had not left. His limbs would not take him away. He felt a heaviness come over him which reached down into his ligaments.

'Am I ill? Am I going to be ill?'

He let his mind jump forward across the years, using the melody that was supposed to take him in the other direction. Balding now, and paunched, he grasped a faceless grey-haired woman around her thickened waist, and slid his polished shoes upon the maple-blocked floor.

> Down Lovers' Lane together
> We'll wander you and I
> Goodbye to stormy weather
> The clouds will soon roll by.

Oh, God, I'd rather die now. If I knew for sure that I'd be selling soft drinks and sun-tan lotion one hundred months from now, I'd want the chandelier to fall and crush my skull. But I will grow old. There's nothing I can do about that. The songs will

113

play, but they will not compensate, cannot assuage. Sentences will be written, by way of art or in trade, and they will make no difference. I am staring down now through the crumbly earth into the pit of my own grave, and the bones of my head are grinning back at me.

A scatter of applause as the singer finished made his scalp itch and tingle, but released his limbs. He turned and walked towards the doors, feeling as though he were pulling himself out of a sticky black tar.

In the doorway, Blackeyes stood, and then was gone.

She had arrived at the wrong moment, just as the band stopped playing. The dancers were leaving the floor, suddenly looking much older than when they were in a musical movement. Their faces, too, snapped shut, as though they knew this themselves. At the tables around the walls, the people leaned their heads in towards each other in small circles of apparent privacy. It was too intimidating for someone much younger, and alone.

Blackeyes walked away down the long, enclosed terrace, between illuminated leaves and chipped white metal. There were decorative tiles on either side of a narrow strip of worn red carpet, and she made her heels clack on them as she veered off the softer material. She was wondering where a smaller bar might be: a couple of vodkas might wash the distant music out of her mind.

'Excuse me – '

Either she did not hear, or, more likely, she chose to take no notice. Jeff hesitated, embarrassed, letting her go on ahead, but the click of her heels, the flow of her glossy black hair, and the slight sway of her walk determined him upon another approach. He caught her up again, and came alongside. Mills and Boon, he thought. *One Enchanted Evening*, he thought. Sticky black tar, he thought. Soft drinks and sun-tan lotion and things which cannot assuage . . .

And Roberts saying, 'before she'd even got her sweet little tongue into a bloody Pina Colada or whatever,' with that snigger waiting behind his face.

Blackeyes did not turn to look at him as he spoke.

'Excuse me, I'm not trying to – to – But aren't you Blackeyes?'

'What about it?' she said, eyes straight ahead, and no break in her walk.

He was conscious of the forward thrust of her firm, bare legs, and of the way the stuff of her skirt clung to the long line of her thigh. A frond of fat, potted plant brushed at his cheek, and behind him the dance band resumed playing. *Remember this!* he thought, wanting to be foolish, wanting to ache.

'I work for Davis Browning Clyde and Roberts,' Jeff said, at her elbow. 'You've got this photo call tomorrow for the Fraggie Bar stuff, haven't you?'

'What about it?'

'It isn't until two o'clock. I thought you were coming down from London on that fast morning train. I didn't know you were staying here tonight as well.'

'As well as what?'

'I mean, as well as – ' Jeff tried to laugh, but his tongue wouldn't roll in his mouth.

She stopped, and faced him.

'What do you want?' she said, and there was no sort of smile to go with the words.

He stuck out his hand, aware of the faint sting of colour at his cheek bones.

'To say hello.'

'Hello.'

She did not take his hand, looked through him, and resumed her walk. The terrace was opening out into the mausoleum of the reception area, where substantial old armchairs with buttoned backs sat waiting for someone to die in them. She went through the double doors. Wap-wap-wap they swung, almost in time to the band as it bounced out another old song behind him.

And fuck you too, he thought.

He turned back, not because he wanted to return to the ballroom, where the proteolytic syncopations would eat out the

115

cells in his head, but because he did not want to look as though he were following her.

You're not much better than a high-class whore, anyway.

The music grew to meet him, and he set his face into a preoccupied expression, as though there were no possibilities of boredom. *Forget this!* he thought, wanting not to be foolish, wanting not to ache.

He swivelled around so quickly that his foot almost slipped on the edging tiles, and ran back along the terrace, barely avoiding an elderly couple who were going to the dance. They looked back at him, angry in a way that pleased both of them, for the prejudice that had unknowingly brought them to this place was being continually reconfirmed.

'Lout!' the old man shouted, relishing an opportunity he would not have dared to take on the open street.

Blackeyes was looking at a glass case near the foot of the wide, curving stairway. It was full of antique silver brooches, some of which were shaped like fish. They should put an aquarium here instead, she was thinking, when the reflection loomed up in the glass as suddenly as a shark in the deeps.

'Would you like to go for a walk?' the glimmer said, as abruptly as its arrival.

She continued to look into the glass, allowing the spurt of alarm to fade back into the reflections that separated the brooches and bangles from the creepy softness and buttoned chairs of the lobby.

'Where to?' she said, and turned to look at him.

He didn't know what to say, and he didn't know how to smile.

'Yuk!' exclaimed Jessica, in a near-retch of disgust that ended, less unpleasantly, in a whoop of derision.

But later that night, listening to the yowling of the cats in the cobbled mews beyong her bedroom window, she stared up at the small tracery of cracks on her ceiling, and changed her mind.

*

Yes, there was a moon hanging in the sky. There was a spangle of stars. A glitter on the sea. And distant music from the great white palace on the shore, seeping out into the summer's night like perfume drifting up from the flowerbeds on either side of the properly tended path as it climbed away from the hotel grounds, approaching and recoiling and creeping back again towards the tufty edge of the cliff. Yes, all of it. A suspicious arrangement.

'But there must be hundreds of self-deceivers like me,' Jeff was saying, his hand almost at her elbow, 'churning out demeaning and vulgar rubbish for even more demeaning and vulgar advertising agencies. And all of us with a novel or a play or a sheaf of poems hidden away in the bottom drawer of our desks. Whose fault is it? Ours! Nobody else's.'

He was not making the most of his opportunity. Circumstance had ordered things better than art, and yet he did not seem to realize how much he was talking, nor that all of it was about himself. Worse, he did not measure how silent she was in the soft darkness, how absorbed in other thoughts.

Ahead of them, as they slowly walked, the hulk of Beachy Head reared up with a hidden groan of effort over the sea. The dance band music from the hotel had faded to nothing. The path lost its smoothness and its neat fringes of flowerbeds, becoming narrower, rougher, and darker.

'What's it about?' she said at last, not quite looking at him.

'My novel?' he laughed, and made a dismissive gesture, a sweep of the hand which, in daylight, might have misled a bird into thinking that food was being offered.

'It's about a middle-aged and disappointed obsessive who cannot stop spying on the young woman who lives next door. He's like an ornithologist. I mean, he has a pair of binoculars and a carefully ruled notebook, tabulating everything about her that he can see. He studies her in her back garden, and through the unfrosted top half of her kitchen window, and as she leaves the house or comes back in, and – that's Beachy Head up there, did you know that?'

She shook her head, making her hair swing: and now she was looking full at him.

'I think it's probably a bit too far to walk,' he said, 'and you haven't got the right sort of shoes. You could easily turn your ankle. They'd never forgive me for that, would they?'

'Does he kill her?'

Their steps had slowed as his account had quickened. They both stopped at the same time, and half-covertly examined each other. He felt an almost overwhelming urge to reach out and touch the line of her face with the tips of his fingers.

'I – ' he began, and then carefully swallowed any following words.

'Don't you know?'

'Oh,' he said, in a tighter voice. 'Oh.'

'What's the matter?'

He held her steady and yet oddly disinterested gaze, then looked quickly away, out over the cliff edge.

'You haven't said a word about yourself,' he said. 'Not a single word.'

'There's nothing to say.'

'Oh, come on – !'

But as he looked back at her, there was a change of light in her eyes, which he understood to be hostility.

'Nothing,' she said, as flat as a flagstone.

As though by mutual consent, or in shared disappointment, they turned back towards the hotel. They did not speak for several hundred yards: and that is more difficult than description makes it seem.

'The band,' he said, when he could bear it no longer.

'Yes,' she said, in a sway that took her a little closer to his side.

The first faint strains of the ballroom music had returned on the night air, with a plangency made doubly melancholy in his mind by the sense of lost opportunity. He looked sidelong at her, and waited for his left foot to go down twice more on the descending path before daring to speak to her again.

'How's anybody going to get to know you?'

'Try fucking,' she said.

She kept on walking, even though he was no longer beside

118

her. He had stopped, with his mouth open, not only because of what she had said, but also because of the unambiguous contempt in its delivery.

Her stride was lengthening, and he let her go.

'Yes!' he shouted after her. 'He *does* kill her!'

21

The corpse of the once lovely young woman had been trundled out of its icy tomb several times for the eyes of the distressed, uncomprehending or fearfully blustering men on the list she had bequeathed to the world, although by now the procedure was not strictly necessary and therefore hardly in order. The identity of what the tabloids still called THE MODEL IN THE POND: NEW REVELATIONS had already been satisfactorily established. The rooms in which she once lived were thoroughly searched. Letters, diaries, greetings cards, and a few strange and barely readable fragments of what the police were for long reluctant to call fiction had been taken away for examination. Various sets of fingerprints were taken from hard surfaces within the rooms. Her clothes had been pawed over. They knew all about her.

Blake showed the body – 'if you would be so good, sir, as to take a careful look' – because he wanted to study the degrees of stress or distaste caused by the first sight of the dead young woman. He thought it possible that she had been murdered: or, if not, that the suicide had been aided and abetted. He was an old-fashioned and in many ways ignorant policeman, and believed that the face caught unawares and before time for adjustment was the window of the soul. Unless it were that of a black man, of course: that was half the trouble in his book – you could never tell for sure what they were up to.

The dead girl bothered him more than any victim he had encountered in years. Her face infiltrated his dreams. He saw her walking naked across the dark and cold grass of the park. Sometimes she turned and spoke, but he could never get hold of what she said.

When they had gone to where she lived, on one of those days where winter suddenly yields its domain, he had felt an utterly inexplicable sadness about a small dapple of sunlight on the wall opposite the narrow windows of the living room. It had been softened only when his eyes had followed the direction of the light and ended on the titles of a row of books. Christ, if that was the sort of thing she read, then no bloody wonder . . .

But he had slipped into his pocket one of the many transparencies of her which they found in a little orange and white box of drawers in the corner of the room. He wondered later why he had done this, for it was an obvious breach of regulations. The impulse to take a picture of her away with him could not be resisted. From time to time when alone, he held it up to the window or to a lamp, and studied it in a deeper and deeper melancholy.

She was almost up to her knees in a smooth blue sea, with her breasts high and bare, her hair loose about her shoulders, and a pout at her sculpted lips.

'Poor little thing,' he said, on several occasions, tasting the salt in the waters.

'What are you doing?' his wife asked, coming unexpectedly into the room. He had turned to look at her with such an ache in his expression that she asked him, instead, whether he had seen the Thermos flask they used to have.

'Why?' he snarled. 'We're not going on a fucking picnic, are we?'

'Not with *you*, that's for sure!' she snapped back, swinging away with a flush at her cheeks, of the kind he had not seen upon her in a decade, and which, earlier still, he used to find entrancing.

Blake put the transparency back into his pocket, and looked at the window again. This time, he could see the dull shine of rain on the row of slate roofs. A rather more explicable grief spun through him in a corkscrew of pain.

You are past fifty, it said. You've had it, old mate.

And this mood had not lessened its desolate grip when, later in the day, he drove thirty miles or so out of London in search of the next name on the list, and bearing upon the set of his shoulders the certainty of vengeance.

*

The river meadows were damp, and splattered here and there with cow pancakes. But the sky was light and almost jovial, with its playful flicks of cloud and different sorts of pale blue in ponds and lagoons of air.

'I think I need another dozen or so buttercups,' the photographer called to one of his assistants, who had cowdung on his boots and an expression which showed that he knew it.

Sitting on the grass, near the fast flow of the swollen river, a girl with dark red hair was cooing and mumbling quietly to herself as she waited for the artificial flowers to supplement the natural abundance all around her. In close upon her, it could have been a sickly Pre-Raphaelite concoction, except for the goose pimples on her bare arms.

The photographer bent down to her, and slightly rearranged the arguably golden hair in its soft cusp at the long white neck.

'Shouldn't be buttercups and daises, should it, angel?' he said to her. 'Orchids and passion-flowers would suit you better.'

'Or-chids,' she chanted, splitting the word because she loved it, and splitting the world because she loved its opiates and chemicals.

'Nigel Bennon? Are you Mr Nigel Bennon?'

The voice was not a cultivated one, and the photographer regarded himself as busy. He was now on his knees in front of the dreamy girl, trying to make her focus on him, away from the far and slow land of wisps and refractions where the river flowed with the sky.

'What of it?' What do you want? Can't you see I'm busy?'

'As a bee,' the model smiled, then repeated the word several times, withdrawing once more.

Blake looked at her, and sniffed back a weary contempt.

'You're a hard man to find, you know that? I've got mud on my wheels and cowshit on my heels. Didn't know you arty-farties had it so tough.'

Bennon stared at him, and then got to his feet. The edge in

122

this man's voice put him on his guard. 'I'm sorry, but I *am* very preoccupied. I'm doing this Arletta Shampoo set of – '

'Police.'

No matter how many times he said it, Blake enjoyed spitting out the word as though it were a pebble he had been sucking.

'Oh,' said Bennon, starting to blink rapidly. 'What do you – ?'

And then he looked at the quietly simpering girl, who was still playing, loose-eyed, with the word 'bee', making it buzz around the nectar of her hair.

'Listen – ,' Bennon said again. 'This girl's condition is not my responsibility – '

'It's the condition of another young lady that is my concern, sir. A former acquaintance of yours, I believe.'

The photographer tried to edge away from the Ophelia at his feet, but Blake had his arms folded and his feet apart, like someone planted in the soggy ground.

'What other – ah – young lady?' Bennon asked, not used to the term.

Blake looked slowly around and about, a gleam in his eyes as though something amused him. An assistant was approaching with a tray of plastic buttercups held before him like things for sale at a football ground. The photographer urged him away with a nervous flutter of his arm.

'Shampoo, did you say?'

Bennon shrugged and gestured, unsure whether to apologize or to boast.

'I see. You got her down by the river here so you can wash her bleed'n hair in it, is that right?'

Surprisingly, the girl laughed: but then, almost immediately, she shivered, hugged herself, and began to rock gently to and fro.

'Sodding coppers.' she said, smiling through drooping strands of hair.

'Get a blanket round her,' Blake said.

'Well, yes, if we're going to have to stop for any – '

'Do you mind if we have a little chat, sir?'

'I – well, if – '

'I suggest we go and sit in one of the vehicles. Yours looks a bloody sight more comfortable than mine, don't it? Sorry to be a nuisance, sir.'

An apparently indignant woman in Wellingtons and an anorak brought a blanket for the model, and the two men walked up the slope of the meadow to where three 'customized' Range-Rovers were parked in line in the muddy lane. They did not speak as they trudged through the clumpy grass, although the now increasingly perturbed photographer kept glancing sideways at the policeman, as though offering his attention. Behind them, the man who had carried the artificial buttercups kicked the tray in petulance, and the girl in the grass laughed until someone shouted at her to shut up.

In the first of the three Range-Rovers, Bennon stared at a photograph, setting his face in puzzled diligence, went to hand it back, looked again as though to make sure, and returned it to Blake.

'Sorry. No. I don't think so – '

'That's interesting,' said Blake. 'Very odd.'

'Sorry – ?'

'Well, you see, sir, I know you know her, oh, know her you certainly do. Intimately, sir,' Blake said, as though he were rehearsing a music-hall routine. 'If you understand my-delicate-use-of that particular phrase. Sir.'

Bennon looked out of the side window, and kept silent.

'Want to see her picture again? Refresh the parts your memory don't reach, eh?'

Bennon shook his head, but did not turn.

'Fair enough,' Blake said, and made a noise with his lips.

They sat in silence for a few moments, each waiting. A few drops of rain pattered suddenly at the windscreen. Blake studied the dashboard dials. Bennon looked out at the droop of the hedgerow.

'Not a very good photograph,' he said, eventually. 'I could do better than that.'

'We know now who she is, or was. Don't you read the papers?'

'Not if I can help it,' Bennon snorted.

'And we know a great deal about her now. Bit by bit. She was also good enough to give us a list of what you *could* call her boyfriends, sir. If you was a quaint old-fashioned flat foot with a weak stomach. Such-as-I.'

'A list.'

'You're not surprised, then? That wasn't a question, was it?'

Bennon shrugged, and looked back at Blake, his eyes glowering.

'In her vagina,' said Blake, meeting the turn of the head with precision.

The photographer crinkled his face, seemed about to speak, but stopped himself. The little squall of rain swept on by, leaving the hedge glistening and trembling.

'I think you know the place, sir.'

Bennon jerked in his seat. His teeth met, and his fist clenched. Blake tensed himself for a blow, even though he knew it would not come.

'We've recovered her diary, and some letters. And some little packets of what isn't castor sugar,' Blake contiinued. 'From her little house.'

'I've never been there,' Bennon said, quickly.

'That's as maybe – '

'No. Never!'

' – but I'd be what you might call very pleased, sir, if you could tell me where you last saw this poor little girl. And where.'

'If I can remember – yes. Of course. But – '

'Would it be by any chance the occasion when you tied her ankles to her wrists and had your fun sort of, sort of arse-backwards? Sir?'

Bennon stared, and slowly shook his head.

'You're out of line,' he said. 'I'm not talking to you. Jesus Christ.'

'Or would it be the time when you supplied her with heroin?'

Bennon stayed silent.

'I'm obliged by an arsehole of a law to read you something, sir.'

'Fuck off, copper.'

'You are not obliged to say anything, sir. But if you do, it is my duty to inform you that anything you say will be noted, and may be used against you in a court of law. Do you understand that, old chap?'

Bennon hesitated, pulled in his breath, then delivered the hint of a nod.

'Then come with me, fuckhead,' Blake said, and did what he had been aching to do since the morning. He slapped the photographer around the side of the head, not so violently as to leave any cuts or bruises, but hard enough to humiliate.

'Put that one down to the poor fucking buttercups,' he said, in a reasonable tone, as the hurt spurted into the photographer's eyes. 'I like the real ones, you see. And a nice little daisy chain to put around your neck, old son.'

22

Jessica looked out of her window upon the yellow door, the fat white tubs, the cobblestones, and fretted about the identity of the callow young man who was the would-be hero, or at least just about the only approximation to a decent man, in the whole of *Sugar Bush*. She could point the finger at everyone else in the book, no matter how swaddled they might be in Kingsley's layers of ignorance and invention. The split between Jamieson and Roberts was a nuisance to her neat mind, but not seriously so. She regarded it as an artistic failure which would not, in the end, compromise the judgement nor lessen the punishment.

Door. Tubs. Stones. Door, tubs, stones. Doortubsstones.

So far as she could remember, she had never described to Kingsley anyone in trousers who remotely resembled 'Jeff', the wet copywriter with the wrong songs in his head. It did not occur to her that her uncle might have made him up. She assumed, unjustly, that the old man had now passed the point where he was still capable of prolonged invention. In her opinion, a rubber undersheet was more likely to be of use to him than a quire of typing paper.

Door, she said. Tubs, she said. Stones.

She raked back over her past, examining the grains.

Well, yes, there *had* been a man attached in some way to one of the bigger advertising agencies who could perhaps be pushed and squeezed and patted into the right configuration. He had smoked a curiously shaped pipe and affected a rough tweed jacket and, once, he had held his head on one side to look at her. The scrutiny had made the colour rush to her cheeks, and yet it had not seemed lascivious or salacious in the ways she was by now beginning to regard as normal.

She could not remember his name.

And, yes, well, yes, he had once interceded on her behalf

when there was a 'misunderstanding' about a job she was supposed to do. Bombed-out, she had missed the pick-up point. Another time, too, he had rebuked a foul little photographer for his sexism and incivility, and she had looked at him out of the corner of her eye, wondering . . .

The door and the stones and the tubs of wilting plants would not yield up his name. But he had not been a copywriter, or, at least, she didn't think so. An artist or a graphic designer, perhaps. She saw charcoal lines on the drawing board, but they refused to join up, and there was no infilling.

'I can't say I care too much for city life, do you?'

This was the only sentence she could recall word for word from those few and brief conversations of eight or nine years ago, the days of what had seemed to her one long acid dream.

I can't say I care too much for city life. I can't say I care too much for city life, do you? Do you? Do *you*? She continued to study the mews houses opposite, then lifted her gaze to the pitch of the slate roof, counting the tiles, and trying out the sentence. What was she going to do with it? One, two, three, four, five, six, seven, eight, nine, ten, eleven, twelve words. That was all! A dozen little tiles to make a man!

But in *Sugar Bush*, and damn each one of its pages, the character Jeff had said nothing which meant 'I can't say I care too much for city life.' On the other hand, he could have worn a tweed jacket of the kind which would graze your face. He could also have had the same soft, sleepily amused eye as – shit! What *was* his name?

On the seventy-third tile, she decided that she might as well call him Jeff after all.

In *Sugar Bush*, he next appeared in shy awkwardness while waiting in the small, thickly carpeted reception area of a photographer's studio. He was too earnestly studying the pictures on the wall, which were almost all of exceptionally beautiful young women, staring back at him with an insolence or an imperiousness that belied, yet ultimately failed to contradict, the essential vulnerability of their youth and their sex.

The blonde girl at the desk, who possessed the sort of face

and figure which might have allowed her on to the hyacinth walls in one of the unframed photographs, smiled to herself at the young man's concentration: it had the nervous intensity of someone who is covering the turmoil in the mind with a steadiness of the eye, as when waiting too long for what one is not in any case very confident of receiving.

'She shouldn't be long now. But you know how it is,' she said.

'That's OK.'

'I told her you were waiting when I went through just now.'

'Oh, you didn't, did you?'

She was amused by his immediate anxiety. 'It's all right,' she said. 'We haven't got a back door. She can't slip away.'

'But – what did she say? I mean – '

'She screamed and tore out a handful of hair. What do you think she said?'

He nodded an acknowledgement of the sardonic and resumed his study of the photographs. This, he thought, has all the potential of a major embarrassment. And there are lots of girls in the world who don't mind being chased, and quite a few who have hitherto been chaste . . . pinion yourself on a bad pun, you misuser of words, he said to himself, trying to take the tension out of his chest.

'Don't say nuffink! I know I'm late!'

Jeff turned from the pictures, startled by the comical vigour of the voice. It was from a busty little blonde cockney, as noisy and colourful as a jewel-eyed macaw shifting on its perch.

'Hello,' said the receptionist. 'You're – ah – ?'

'Marilyn Monroe. Who do you fink I am? I'm the one who's bleed'n late, that's who I am.'

'Rosie Hughes.'

'That's me to a T,' the model said, addressing Jeff now. 'On time for the grotty jobs. Too late for the ones with a bit of class. It's the same with me blokes.'

Jeff smiled politely, but wondered why she was talking to him, and looking at him with such an unabashed appraisal.

'Oo are you, then? Male model, are you?'

'No,' he said, half-way to being indignant.

'Fought not,' she beamed, unreasonably pleased.

'Rosie – ' the receptionist tried.

'Shall I go on frew or what?' Rosie asked, turning her china-doll face back to the girl at the desk. 'Expect he'll have his bleed'n tizz in a whizz, won't he?'

Without pause for breath, she swung her breasts back to Jeff: or, at least, that is what he felt had happened.

'This bugger tried to fob me off wiv green bananas, didney!'

'Sorry?' he said.

'What *you* sorry for, love? Wasn't you that done it, was it?'

He was totally lost, and could do nothing but grin like a fool.

'Rosie – ' the receptionist tried again, as the girl held up a plastic bag, a look of childlike affront in her baby blue eyes.

'Geezer down the market,' she said. 'Hiding the green ones under the ripe ones. Listen, mate, I sez – if you think *I'm* green as well –!'

The door at the back had opened, and Jeff, still trying to adjust his face to whatever might be appropriate, saw Blackeyes come through. The swallow at his throat was enough to make Rosie turn her tornado of an attention once more.

'Hello, love!' she said, without a break.

'Hi,' returned Blackeyes, in her flat voice, and then, warming, 'oh. Hi!'

'Gawd! You ain't half doing well, entcha? Picture all over the place! See – I told you! You're better off without bloody great knockers like mine!'

The ebullience and unselfconsciousness made everyone laugh.

'This your bloke?' Rosie asked, pleased by the responses, and seeing the unchanged direction of Jeff's eyes.

'Yes,' Blackeyes said, without looking at him.

'No,' Jeff said, at the same time, taking his gaze off her.

Rosie looked from one to the other with open interest.

'Don't make up your minds in a hurry. There's always plenty of time – '

130

'Rosie!' thundered a voice, from the photographer in the open doorway.

'Oh God,' she said, with a roll of the eyes.

'There *isn't* always plenty of time. You are late! You've thrown the whole session out of the window! Now, please, please, please. Are you ready for work, or are you not?' boomed the gentlemanly voice, issuing from a small, pale, and almost elderly man with hands not unlike pigeons in flight.

'It was this bloke down the market – ' Rosie was explaining, with a different set of gestures, as Blackeyes and Jeff, with oddly covert glances at each other, walked down the narrow stairs and into the street.

When Jeff began to laugh, a few paces along the pavement, it was more out of anxiety than amusement. Blackeyes had said nothing to him, and he felt ridiculously unsure about whether he was walking with her, or merely, and almost coincidentally, alongside her.

'What's funny?' she said, with a dart of a glance.

'Bloody great knockers like mine,' he laughed, imitating Rosie.

His laughter fed on itself and quickly expanded into helpless inanity, so that he had to stop, shoulders bouncing like a trampoline, and throw his head back to let out the roar.

She stood, looking at him, at first with a smile, and then not.

'I'm sorry,' he gasped, wiping at his eyes. 'It's not that funny, is it?'

'No,' she said, discouragingly.

She was still looking at him in the same way: curious, as though he might be another species rather than simply another sex; questioning; potentially contemptuous, and undoubtedly wary.

My bounty is as boundless as the sea, My love as deep, he wanted to say, or 'What's the matter, my love?' or 'Can I please touch your face?'

'She amused me, that's all,' he actually said, lamely.

'Why did you wait for me? What do you want?'

'To – talk?'

'What about?'

Hope, maybe. Faith. The sweet possibility of Constancy?

'Well – ' he pretended to search the heavens, falling back upon the cowardice of comedy. 'I suppose we could talk about chocolate, or the Bomb, or we could find out whether we like Brahms or pasta – '

He thought he saw the trace of a smile or signs of tolerance in those too steady eyes, and was encouraged enough to be more like the person he considered himself to be, which was drawn out of the buried image of a brave soul walking a long white road towards some city of gold.

'No,' he said. 'I don't want to talk about those things. Not yet, anyway. I don't want there to be an agenda. I'd like to get to know you, please. I'd like *you* to talk. I mean, I'd like us to talk to each other.'

She nodded, and then continued walking. Her reflection darkly glimmered for a moment in the large window of a store displaying office computer systems. Mildly encouraged, he followed, and walked beside her, passing beyond the modern prayer-wheels and alongside a newsagent's, where a rack of magazines showed her reflection again, but in coloured photographs.

Even as he walked, so close to the sway of her hip, so near to the high bone of her cheek, one part of his mind shouted objection and another heard again fat-faced Roberts' dirty jokes. He looked at her, but kept silent, for he could see that she was in a turmoil of thought.

What she was doing was trying not to step on any of the cracks between the slabs of paving stone: and to do anything so complicated as that needed concentration.

Door. Tub. Stones. Door, tub, stones.

Jessica sucked her mind back from the silent pair walking the long pavement and brooded again on the possible relationship between the half-remembered man in the tweed jacket and the young copywriter who imagined himself approaching a city of gold. She knew that all such places, magical in each distant prospect, emptied their buckets of sewage over the walls. The gates stayed locked, so that all you got at the end of your pilgrimage was a splatter of filth.

She stayed at her window a few minutes longer, inhabiting words.

'Hope, maybe. Faith. The sweet possibility of Constancy,' went into her head, without the qualifying twist of the question mark, the most human of all punctuations.

> *My bounty is as boundless as the sea,*
> *My love as deep*

It was not Kingsley's habit, in his prose, to attribute his many quotations, so she did not know where the lines properly belonged.

Worse still, she did not know where 'Jeff' himself properly belonged. The whispers of memory which so faintly spoke at the back of her mind were more like a tickle of breath in the hairs of the ear than the shapes of actual words. She had the sensation, but not the sense, of her own past imparting information to her.

Jessica spun quickly back into the room, and her hand plunged to the telephone.

'Uncle Maurice?'

'Who is calling?'

He always said this, even though she was the only living person who could call him uncle.

'It's Jessica – '

'Oh, Jessica, my dear. I thought you had abandoned me, but I can't – '

'I want to talk to you about someone in *Sugar Bush*,' she said, too quickly.

'My dear Jessica. I can't talk to you now. I am being interviewed,' he said grandly. 'I have a young man here in my abode who represents *KRITZ* magazine. There is a photographer, too, who is taking pictures of me, for some reason I find hard to fathom.'

Oh, you old fart. You pompous driveller!

'Really?' she said, instead.

'I'm told they want to put my portrait on the cover, Jessica.

133

Even as I speak to you across the wasteland of decaying city streets, the young man is continuing to take pictures of me holding this instrument, and the other young man continues to record my voice on his little machine, no doubt in the hope of catching some stray aphorism. Apparently, I am on my way to being a cult, my dear. Like the yo-yo and the pogo stick before me, no doubt.'

'Uncle Maurice – '

'So you see, my dear. I cannot discuss my book with you at the moment – '

My book, *my* book. You disgusting old thief!

'I thought it was time I cooked you a nice meal again, Uncle.'

'Yes?'

'I'm doing a Malayan curried chicken with pepper, onions, coconut cream, all that, and I'm following it with celestial pineapple.'

'Celestial pineapple?'

'Lychees and balls of melon and chunks of pineapple in a pineapple shell. I thought it's a pity not to share it. I'll send a taxi for you, shall I? At, say, half-past six?'

She knew that he would be hesitant about seeing her again, but the oriental bait lay too deliciously in the trap. Sweet, sweet and sour. He agreed, of course he agreed, and then suddenly broke the connection with an odd gasp. When she tried to ring back, he was engaged, or he had left his phone off the hook.

134

23

'Jeff sat unrelaxed on a small white sofa in a small white room, watching sliced shapes of her through a white venetian blind that separated the tinier kitchen from the living area. She was making tea. A faint smell of bergamot oil came through the slats, and he felt his throat tighten. He wanted to remember everything, but his senses would not co-operate. Each door into his soul was shutting, one after the other, so that he was locked in with his own tremulous anxieties. A day later, and he could not even remember how the walk in near silence along the pavement had led to this room. Had they taken a bus? A taxi? He could not unravel the journey, nor find the little rift within the lute . . .'

Kingsley's account characteristically dropped in five words from Tennyson, unacknowledged and, in context, meaningless. The vapours of his prose were more like friar's balsam than the bergamot oil, but no matter how many orifices were made to stream, the tale of the doomed young woman had steadily climbed the best-seller lists.

It ill becomes the present writer to make snide remarks about his elderly colleague, for I have used the old fellow's narrative as the basis of my own account: and what an effort it has been, I can tell you, to remove the excesses of language, the glancing quotations plundered from better works, the sententious redundancy of such phrases as 'each door into his soul was shutting'.

Jessica, trying to do the same thing, was not up to it.

The few sentences she contrived to get out of her head and on to the page were so distorted by indignation or an even worse hatred that one failed to notice their other deficiencies. She seemed to have no idea of how to construct a paragraph, a piece of standard literary engineering as necessary to a writer as – but, no, I have recently been told that I too easily or readily pontificate, even that I am at times sanctimonious, so I will desist.

The point is, she couldn't do it. And, in my opinion, the realization was driving her, fast, towards the very rim of insanity. Perhaps she had crossed it already, but not so far that she could not be brought back. But by what means?

Once I had asked the question, I knew that the answer had to be a matter of accident, or, if you want a more comforting word, coincidence.

And how, not being God, and with other chickens to feed, how am I going to arrange *that*, since accident and design are mutually contradictory?

24

I remember that I felt as stiff as a log as I sat on the little sofa in her living room, watching her make tea through the slats of the blind which came down to the cupboards, separating off the kitchenette from the rest of her space. It hardly seemed possible that I was here at all. I had thought about her so much, and invented so many imaginary conversations, that now I had the chance to put some of them into play, so to speak, my brain clogged itself up with a wholly sexual tension.

She was so beautiful that I felt a sort of vertigo when I looked at her. The feeling you get when the lift goes down too fast.

'It's funny,' she was saying, moving about behind the blind, 'but I never used to like tea. Now I love it.'

'What sort of tea is it?' I asked, and I'm sure my voice didn't sound right.

She came out from behind the blind, carrying a tray.

'Earl Grey,' she said.

I can't say that I care for tea very much, but when I do have a cup I like to put plenty of milk in it. I knew you were not supposed to do that with Earl Grey. Even now, I remain astonished that such small irritations can be registered by a mind that was apparently so incapable of producing a truly coherent thought. As I accepted the cup, which had no milk in it, I knew that I was not going to do myself justice.

'This is very nice,' I said, and nearly spilt some.

'Do you have any sugar?' I also said.

'Oh, do you take sugar?'

About to sit down opposite me, she straightened and moved back towards her little kitchen.

'I'm not sure I have any – '

'It's all right,' I said. 'No. Really. Sometimes I do, and, and, sometimes I – don't.'

But she was opening and shutting the overhead cupboards, looking for the stuff, saying she *thought* she had some, but, since she never used it, and so on, and so forth, that I felt in some way culpable, like a smoker in a house with no visible ashtrays.

By the time she sat down again, with apologies, I would have drunk the Earl Grey with a dessertspoonful of salt in it.

'Actually,' I said, my lips to the cup, 'I think it really does taste nicer without sugar. You're right.'

She sat there looking at me, big eyes over the rim of her own cup. Her chair was higher than the one-and-a-half seater I was in, so I had a terrific view of her long and slender legs. It almost made up for the regret I felt that she had not squeezed in next to me on the tiny white sofa. Hip to hip would have suited me fine.

Since she stayed so unnervingly silent, and because I did not know how to make whatever conversation there might be tilt in my direction, I looked around the room, desperate for something to take my eye.

'This is very nice,' I said, claiming first prize for originality.

She didn't give me a blue ribbon. I would have to work harder.

'Small is beautiful,' I added. Beat that, Schumacher.

'It's just for me,' she said. 'Nobody else comes here.'

'What? Never?'

'You're the first,' her eyes still looking at me over the rim of her cup.

This ought to have been the moment when I simply smiled back at her and relaxed my limbs. Failing anything so sensible as that, I could at least have changed the subject. But, no. My face went into a helpless spasm which was supposed to represent a manly or sophisticated variant of pleasure, but which must have looked like a leer.

'So-o,' I said instead, rolling the tempting vowel like a German POW Camp Commandant (with a K) in an old British film. 'I've penetrated the inner sanctum.'

The fugitive softness or near-shyness on her beautiful face

instantly flitted out of my reach. The good Lord God couldn't have dealt with Lot's wife's zygomaticus any quicker. Bang! She put her cup down so hard on the chess-squared little table beside her that it went *chink* in the nasty way, I've always imagined, that alligators close their teeth. And I still can't work out exactly what was supposed to be so offensive in what I had said.

'I get fucked other places,' she snapped, in tones which one would normally describe as primly affronted.

I didn't say anything.

'Hotel rooms. Mostly,' she added, looking hard at me.

Perhaps I should have clacked my china down, too, but there didn't seem to be anywhere convenient to put it. Theatrical gestures are not in my line, and this is rarely out of sweet equanimity but mostly because events or places or furniture arrangements conspire to prevent them. Awkwardness moderates all passions. I held on to my saucer.

'Um,' I said, and my lips stuck on it

'Many?' I asked after that, repelled and excited in about equal measures.

'Many times,' she said, frowning now.

'I mean – ' I said, trying to stop my furtive eyes from sliding off my face, 'I mean, men. I mean, many men – ?'

'Yes. Many.'

I looked at the ceiling and I looked at the floor, which is nothing particularly spectacular – except I think I managed to do both these things at the same time.

'I've lost count,' she added, with no sign of bravado.

If she had tilted her nose or widened her mouth when saying this, I don't think I could have sipped another drop of her sour brew, nor spoken any other words except those needed to get out of the room. But, no, there seemed to be something else behind her eyes: the merest quiver of anxiety, or a sort of veiled plea. Also, she had let me in to this place, which might mean that she needed a listener.

My bounty is as boundless as the sea . . .

She kept looking at me, and I sat there thinking of the oceans, ho ho. I managed not to say anything foolish, principally because I wasn't able to say anything at all. *Lost count?* Believe me, it's a lie when people say that tea tastes better without milk and sugar in it: the stuff was going down my throat like boiled nightshade berries.

She still kept looking at me.

'Nice tea,' I croaked.

'But I don't bring anyone here,' she said, as though about to reach out with her hand. 'This is my cave.'

'What? No cave men, then?'

It was supposed to be a joke. An attempt to lighten the atmosphere, et cetera. One day there is going to be a conversation-stopper of a book called *The Collected Asides of Jeff Richards*.

'What I do or don't do with my own life is my own affair, all right?' she said, withdrawing the hand I thought she had been almost ready to offer.

My bounty was not so boundless that I wanted to drink any more of her damned Earl Grey. I put the cup on the floor and pressed my lips together. She took her gaze off me, and moved it towards the window, where the light coming through reminded me for some reason of a dreadful old hymn.

We sat in silence for so long that I inadvertently allowed the little pellet of misery I had been carrying around with me to start to swell, and swell, and then swell.

'Oh, Christ,' I said, but probably none too clearly, for she didn't look around.

I wanted to get up, but I didn't seem to be able to move.

'If you want to go to bed, that's all right by me,' she said. 'Otherwise – '

'Otherwise what?'

'Otherwise let me be.'

Any invitation to do some bonking with a girl who looks like she looks would be the cherry on the cupcake, and I couldn't understand the limp indifference of the one bit of me which would have to do the work. This was not a matter of honour or decency or fastidiousness, or any of those sorts of mask. I simply could not respond. But I did laugh. I mean, out loud. A real laugh.

'You poor cow,' I said, when I had finished. 'You poor bloody idiot.'

She stood up, and then sat down. I don't remember ever before seeing someone quite so puzzled.

'Let's talk,' I suggested, only just keeping down another bizarre whoop.

'What about?'

'You.'

'No, thank you.'

'Me, then.'

'No. Thank you.'

So we sat there for a bit longer, opposite each other. Her long legs gleamed in the fading light. Her big eyes shone, too, but I didn't know with what. The tea went cold. Thank goodness.

'How about my book,' I suggested. 'We could talk about that.'

Pretty neat, considering that I had not really written a word of it. But if you talk about a story, sooner or later you are going to have to talk about yourself . . .

It's the little rift within the lute, that by and by will make the music mute: even when the song is called 'Clementine'.

25

The last complete day of her life before Blackeyes drowned herself in cold water was brisk and bright under a high lemony sky flecked with little clouds so frisky that they were almost pink. She spent the working hours of it in the countryside between Hayward's Heath and Maresfield, in Sussex. Bare trees showing white in the sharp air brought out the worst in Maurice James Kingsley's prose. For a page or two, he indulged himself in the style of one of the great Russians, who make your heart ache for a landscape you have never seen. He was also winding himself up for the delicious despairs which were so soon to follow.

Melancholy sentences at odds with a day brimming over with laughter thinned themselves down to an empty country road and then to a grated private track, where a group of figures with intent faces had gathered around a large German motorcycle. They were a film crew, spoiling the bright air with oaths and gesticulations.

'But I'm telling you, I don't know how to ride this thing,' Blackeyes was protesting, straddled above the menacing, silver-coloured cylinders.

'Darling,' the director gestured. 'Dar-ling! Stop it!'

She was wearing little silver-studded boots, a black leather skirt too short for decency, and a pale blouse that might as well have been made out of cling-film. Her nipples thrust themselves into two silver stars of the kind formerly worn by Texas Rangers. The regulation helmet enclosing her black hair in a carapace of silver completed the appearance of a sex-obsessed alien from some libertine planet beyond the restraints of the solar system.

'I can't,' she said, in robotic tones, a degenerate refusing to play.

'Darling! Listen to me! Darling, they *told* you it was going to be a motorbike. I made absolutely sure the agency told you. What did you think it was going to be? Fucking roller-skates?'

'I can't,' she said, monotonously.

'What do you mean?' the director asked, as though she had not been repetitive.

'I don't know how to ride it.'

The director turned away, spreading his open palms.

'Bert,' he commanded. 'Show her. For Christ's sake, show her.'

The subordinate Bert pulled up his attention from her thighs. 'You know how to ride a bike, eh? An ordinary push-bike?'

'No,' she said.

'Didn't think you would. Somehow, I didn't think you would.'

The director folded his arms, unfolded them, and looked up at the sky.

'Blackeyes,' he said. 'What is really the matter? I mean, you've done nothing but complain since we got here. So – come on – what's wrong, darling?'

'I don't know how to ride this thing.'

She kept on saying it, in lifeless tones, looking directly at none of the figures around her. A recalcitrant child on the edge of a tantrum, or so they all thought. Bert's explanation of how to kick down was interrupted in the same voice, using the same words: I don't know how to ride this thing. I don't know how to ride this thing.

'Shut up!' the director yelled, after several minutes of this.

This time, she took her eyes from the middle-distance, and looked straight at him.

'Can I say something? Will you listen to me?' she asked.

'Yes,' he said, eagerly. 'Yes. Of course.'

'I don't know how to ride this thing.'

They stared at each other. 'Fuck,' the director said, very quietly. 'Fuck,' he said again, a little louder. 'Fuck! Fuck! Fuck!' he yelled, making his hands into claws.

'*We're ready here any time you are,*' interrupted a megaphoned

143

voice from further down the road. The director unclenched his hands, and put his face close to her helmeted head.

'I'm going to give you a signal,' he said. 'And then I want you to – '

'I don't know how to ride this thing,' she interrupted.

'Then get off it!'

'Sure.'

She swung her studded boots off the machine without argument, and stood beside it, apparently searching the horizon.

'Blackeyes,' the director said. 'Will you please get back on that bike?'

'What?'

'Get on the fucking bike, you bitch!'

'Sure,' she said, but with a new glint in her eye.

She sat on the saddle again, and stared straight ahead. The director folded his arms, unfolded them, looked at Bert, looked down the road where the others waited, and cleared his throat.

'Blackeyes,' he said. 'I'm having no more of this shit from you or anybody else. Do you finally understand that? Are you with me?'

'Sure.'

'No more. Right? None!'

'Right.'

'I shall raise my arm and then when I drop it, you will rev up this machine. That's one. Two, I shall raise my arm again, and then when I drop it again, you will come down the road full throttle straight at – '

She had started to shake her head, and he struggled to maintain what he thought to be the new authority in his voice.

'Straight down the road, as though straight at us and – '

'I don't know how to ride this thing.'

Bert let out a laugh, but swallowed it as he looked at the director, whose face seemed to be changing shape, collapsing inwards so that it resembled the front of a dessert spoon with bits of pale blancmange sticking on it.

'You bitch,' he said. 'You bitch.'

144

In the small silence that followed, a wood pigeon began its dreary coo, very near. Blackeyes continued to look at some distant point, without a flicker. Tears sprang into the director's eyes, and, like a figure in a dream, he slowly pulled back his arm and made a fist of his hand.

'Hey,' said Bert, alarmed.

'Shut your bloody mouth!' the director screamed, but broke the spring of the blow that had been about to swing.

'Who the fuck do you think you are? Bloody Hitler or something?' said Bert.

The director turned away with an odd noise, took several deep breaths, and then appeared to study the raggedy fringe of stripped trees where the wood pigeon so softly moaned. He heard it as the sound of his own humiliation.

'We're ready when you are!' repeated the megaphone, causing alarm to several other birds. A flutter of black went up from the trees.

'Blackeyes,' the director said, not looking at her. 'I don't want to be nasty. I don't want to be insulting. No way. What I'm going to do is walk back along this track, and wait for you to drive this machine, OK?'

He did not wait for an answer, but marched off down the private road towards the rest of the crew, his head held up like a soldier, and his arms swinging.

'Bitch,' he said to himself as the left foot went down, and 'Bitch' again as the right foot followed.

Bert watched him go, then put his hand on Blackeyes: her leg, inevitably.

'Better try and do it, love, else that little shit'll have a heart attack, eh?'

He squeezed her exposed thigh, as though this were a routine perk, and then he saw the damp glitter at her eyes and took his hand away.

'Hey,' he said, obscurely ashamed.

She continued to look at the horizon, but now large tears formed and rolled down her cheeks, giving her the appearance of a child distressed because her fancy dress was not suitable for the party.

'Hey,' Bert said again. 'It's no big deal, love. Christ, it don't matter, do it?'

Blackeyes wept, and yet her eyes stayed steady and her face did not crumple.

'I don't care,' he thought he heard her say, as she kicked down hard and the big motorbike roared into life. She twisted the grips, and bent down low to hug the machine.

Half-way along on his indignant march, one two, one two, the director stopped at the shattering noise, and smiled in blessed relief. As he turned to look back, he saw a beast out of hell hurtling towards him. Astonishment instantly expanded into fear, and he threw himself headlong from the narrow road into a straggle of winter bushes. The motorbike thundered past him, to distant cheers from the crew, and an unheard cackle of incredulity from Bert.

The cheers ended when it became apparent that she was not going to stop. She swerved around the camera, scattering those nearest to it, and continued in a souped-up snarl of engine power along the remainder of the private road and out through the gates, bump, bump over a ridge of grass and on to the country road edged by taller trees. The sound flattened out and bounced back and then faded away, so that the indignant twitter of the birds could be heard again. She had gone.

The director sat on his backside in the bushes, staring in a stupefied fashion at his grazed and bloodied palms, and torn knee. He realized that he would probably have to abandon that day's schedule, which would do him no good at all. The after-shave commercial would be done on another occasion, and by somebody else. He would have to lecture for a little longer at the film school than he had hoped: fortunately, his subject gave him no trouble there, because he knew how easily difficult the synthesis between semiology and Marxism could be made to appear.

26

An irritated New Journalist sat on the edge of Kingsley's rumpled bed, pulling at the ring in his ear as he watched his colleague plunder all of the old man's attention.

'Now just look at the lens, OK?' the young photographer was saying. 'Don't move an inch until I tell you.'

'Polite little beast, aren't you?' Kingsley glowered, but he was not genuinely offended, for he had picked up no verbal echoes of a scene in his own book, and no longer felt afraid in the way he had a little earlier.

'We all have to do things we don't want to sometimes, Mr K,' Colin said, busily clicking.

Mark made a tut-tutting noise, as much against the washerwoman remark as in an expression of his own impatience. He had marshalled a few questions in his mind which he felt sure would throw the old chap into a tizz, and expose him for a plagiarist and a posturing fraud.

'Look,' said Colin, annoyed by the tutting, 'why don't you just ask him what you want? I'm not interfering, am I?'

'And I haven't got all day,' Kingsley added, almost visibly puffing himself up.

'Ah, but what's a day, sir?' Mark said, seeing an opening. 'You've been silent for such a long, long time, entcha?'

'I am not a hack,' Kingsley said, grandly. 'The mere fact that I wait awhile between publications for the Muse is no – '

'Twenty-seven years, ennit?'

'Look straight at the lens,' Colin ordered.

'Why did you stop? Did something happen to you?'

'That's it,' said Colin. 'That's a good face, the growly one.'

'Colin!' Mark yelled.

'A poetic sensibility cannot be commanded up at will, *ex nihilo*,' Kingsley said, concentrating now on the young man sitting on the bed, and feeling faint tremors of potential danger. 'And anyway *Strangers Unaware* is still very much in print. Furthermore, it's on the examination syllabus now, you know. Hundreds of poor little buggers have to keep it in their desks, eh? Get out your Maurice James Kingsley, turn to page eighty-four, all that sort of stuff, eh? By Christ, there must be an awful lot of snotty-nosed little bastards growing up with a deep and abiding hatred of me.'

'But that book was a long time ago, wasn't it?'

Kingsley did not want to answer questions of this kind, and was disappointed that what he considered to be an amusing diversion had neither worked nor induced a smile. The earnest expression in Mark's eyes troubled him. He had seen the same sort of look many times in his life, and knew it to be a threat.

'Imagination,' he blustered, tapping his forehead. 'Imagination! You are talking about a work of imagination. It comes from *here*, sir. Not the pages of a calendar.'

Fortunately, the telephone rang: a less rare event than it used to be before *Sugar Bush* had made its way in the world. Mark took the chance to jerk his head at Colin, indicating that the photographer should get out of the way. Colin looked blankly back, then turned to stare out of the window.

'Who is calling?' Kingsley was saying to the telephone, as though he were a very grand butler to an enormously grand Himself. And then he looked across, furtively, at Mark.

'My dear Jessica, I can't talk to you now. I am being interviewed. I have a young man here in my abode who represents *KRITZ* magazine. There is a photographer, too, who is taking pictures of me, for some reason I find hard to fathom.'

Oh, you old fart, thought Mark. You pompous driveller!

He shifted his position on the edge of the bed, more to give at least minimal physical expression to his contempt for the inflated telephone talk than to get comfortable. There was something hard and lumpy sticking into the bottom of his back.

'Even as I speak to you across the wasteland of decaying city streets,' Kingsley was booming, looking now, and less furtively, at the approaching Colin, 'the young man is continuing to take

148

pictures of me holding this instrument, and the other young man continues to record my voice on his little machine, no doubt in the hope of catching some stray aphorism . . .'

More like, catch some stray disease, thought Mark, shifting his backside again and noticing the unsavoury pale grey of what must once have been the white undersheet.

Oh, my God!

His scalp prickled, and he held his breath. There was something brown and furry sticking out from beneath the bedclothes, disturbed by his fidgets.

'Celestial pineapple?' Kingsley was saying, mysteriously, his mouth moistening.

Mark surreptitiously pulled at the thing in the bed, his momentary alarm subsiding, to be replaced by an inner whoop of hilarity as he saw what it was. He lifted up the battered little teddy bear, and sat it on his knee: and both he and the toy seemed to have identically solemn expressions, the single ear-ring matching the single brown eye.

Turning slightly, with a faint gleam of spittle on his lips as he accepted the invitation to dine on Malayan chicken with pepper, onions and coconut cream, Kingsley saw his little chickadee faithlessly astride the young man's baggy trousered knee. He dropped the telephone, and began to tremble with a humiliation he knew had been so long postponed but was always inevitable – inevitable – inevitable . . .

The word tolled each syllable, and again, and again, like a heavy bell in the otherwise catastrophically emptied-out belfry of his head.

'Lookie here,' said Mark, with a smirk, jiggling the teddy on his knee.

Kingsley put his hands up to his ears, and then, in a tell-tale twitch of indecision, clamped one of them to his mouth, as though he were about to be violently sick. The two young men stared at him.

'Oh, poor liddool thing!' said Colin, redirecting his camera. 'It's only got one eye!'

The click of the camera silenced the bell in Kingsley's head, and released his elderly limbs. He pushed Colin out of the way with the palms of his hands, and plucked the teddy bear from Mark's knee.

'Leave her alone. Leave her be!' he croaked. 'You have no right to – this is none of your – '

He hugged the teddy bear tightly to his chest, rocking in distress, the words giving way to a strange, mewing anguish which caused the two visitors from *KRITZ* magazine to look hesitantly at each other and then not at each other in their embarrassment.

In a minute, Kingsley seemed to realize the picture he made. He stopped rocking and forced the noises of distress so hard back down his throat that they could see his Adam's apple bob in vigorous protest within its cage of sinew.

'You shitbags,' he gasped.

He allowed the teddy bear out of his suffocating hug, and held it limply dangling by one of its arms.

'Mr Kingsley – ' Mark began, not knowing how to continue.

'An artefact,' Kingsley announced, only the wildness in his eyes showing how much he had lost control of himself. 'An artefact from the past. A genuine residue of the dear dead days.'

He held out the teddy, inviting them to look at it, and then let it drop with a small, dull thud to the bare boards of the floor.

'An object,' he said, with some of the boom returning, 'thrown up in the course of diligent research for my next book. I am in this instance the soldier home from the wars, with his sword at his side and his knapsack on his back. The reference will no doubt escape you, for you both seem remarkably ill educated.'

Colin snorted so deeply in his nose and throat that no one else could have determined whether the noise was one of pleasure or indignation.

'And now,' said Kingsley, putting his foot on the fallen teddy as though he had just shot it, 'I would like your apologies for harbouring such juvenile asininities as the thoughts you both appear to have entertained in this, my own humble abode. Please deliver them on your way out.'

'Mr Kingsley,' Mark said again, standing up from the treacherous bed.

'Please be careful when you leave not to step in the dog shit on the pavement, a piece of advice I am always prepared to give to those who too obviously need it,' Kingsley said, removing his foot from the teddy, and turning away to one of his windows, where he folded his arms, sighed deeply, and stared out, his back to them.

'One to one,' Colin said to Mark, maliciously delighted. 'This is symbiosis.'

Kingsley remained at the window, looking down at the far pavement, and did not speak or show any sign of turning as the two young men briefly hit out at each other before gathering up their things and leaving.

He listened for the door to bang shut, and strained to hear the receding slap of their feet on the stone steps of the stair down to the shabby entrance. Eventually, he was able to see them in the street, walking together as though they were the best friends in the world, and stopping every few yards to double up with laughter.

The tension ebbed away from him, leaving a flat shore of melancholy. The street and the buildings opposite faded from his vision. He saw instead the creamy moon and the glistening stars of a summer night, with the car he used to have parked a little way behind him on the grass at the side of a rural track.

O My Darling, O My Darling
O My Darling Clementine
You are gone and lost forever
Lost forever, Clementine.

When he at last turned back into the big, darkening room, his eyes streaming so much that big drops dangled on the end of his nose, the teddy bear was nowhere to be seen.

27

The anomalous and the implausible niggled in flashes of nerve within Jessica as she steadily chopped the already cooked chicken into small pieces. Her scheme could never achieve perfect symmetry because the season was out of sequence. Deconstruct though she might, putting the truth back into Kingsley's subversions, it remained the case that September was not winter. The leaves were still rich upon the boughs, and in pockets of the city you could smell the dampness at the roots. A novelist can insist upon the height or colouring of a character, and describe the pattern on a chair, but need not be believed. It is more difficult to ignore precise descriptions of bare trees and ground that is hard and misted with frost.

The chicken had lain on the plate in a way that reminded her (as most things did) of what it was like to be a woman in a world commandeered by men. No – she corrected herself – of what it was like to be 'beautiful' and young and female in such a slaughterhouse. She saw lines of chickens hung up by hooks, passing along a row of men in aprons, and the shed was thick with feathers.

> Chick, chick, chick, little chicken
> Lay a little egg for me.

Jessica decided that she would have to decree changes in the climate. Why not? she thought, bearing hard down with the knife. Why can't I play God, too?

When she had finished chopping, and assembling the other materials, she looked at the clock and saw that she could sit down and think things through for another three-quarters of an hour. But first, a drink. A drink!

'She lay on the sofa, the vodka on the small table beside her, a pale figure in a white room. It was as though she were posed there, wanting the set of her head and the slender flow of her arm to be seen. Her body had always said Look At Me.'

Thus it was that Kingsley had opened the last chapter of *Sugar Bush*, observing that both the arrangement of the room and the fading of the light at its small windows were propitious for contemplation. A distant chime from the clock on the palace in the park entered so softly into the mind of Blackeyes that she was aware of it only as a tinge of sadness: and so it was, now, with Jessica.

'She is like a reflection of me, but a reflection in water, and not a mirror,' Jessica said, out loud, to hear what the words sounded like.

She drank some of her vodka. Blackeyes had done the same. She turned her face towards the back of the sofa, as Blackeyes once did. Both of them closed their eyes, and listened to the whispers, 'with grave attention and steadfast application', as Kingsley said of the young woman he thought he had invented.

Jessica saw herself walking across the grass towards the pond, her hair swaying on her shoulders. She sat up with a jerk, and stared almost wildly around her room, before deciding that she must have slipped into sleep. But the clock showed that no more than a minute had passed, and she shuddered, sensing escape from the old man's dream.

Onions and garlic had to be stir fried in very hot oil, but that, by definition, would take less than another minute.

Why do I keep looking at the clock? Why do I feel so tense?

She knew that she knew, but held off the acknowledgement, because thinking about what must in justice be done would only make it more difficult to accomplish without false intrusions of guilt and nausea. Better to deal with the dismembered chicken before cooking the goose!

There was still time to look once more at the last chapter of *Sugar Bush*, even though she already knew it word for word. It was the arrangement of the sentences which had to be changed if Blackeyes were to be saved.

'The water came over her shining boots, swallowed up her

knees and long thighs, and then made a line around the naked swell of her belly,' the last paragraph had claimed. 'In next to no time, there was nothing but her head to be seen, then a few thick strands of floating black hair, and soon she was completely submerged, with no sign of fuss or struggle. Whatever traces she may have left on the lives of others, this girl, she had gone now without a ripple. The water smoothed itself flat, and reflected back the sky.'

Jessica finished her drink with an almost violent gesture, then went to the shelves, where she had to click on an angled light to make the spines glow. 'Without a ripple,' she muttered. 'Without a ripple.'

The light fell across the dimpled face of a china doll propped up on its frilly bottom at the end of the shelf, in the least-used corner of the room. She had kept it since her childhood, and still addressed it from time to time, using the name she had always used, which was Clementine.

She had no eye for the doll at this moment. *Sugar Bush* was taken from the shelf, where it was sandwiched between a novel called *Laughter In The Dark* and another volume in fierce black and red covers called *The Myth Of Women's Masochism* which she had only recently purchased. Although it, too, was a new publication, the pages of *Sugar Bush* looked as worn, as marked, and as torn as a book salvaged from some long-gone circulating library.

'Without a ripple,' she repeated, with an edge, as she took the novel back to the sofa and lay down again.

'She lay on the sofa, the vodka on the small table beside her, a pale figure in a white room,' Jessica read. 'It was as though she were posed there, wanting the set of her head and the slender flow of her arm to be seen. Her body had always said Look At Me, although she had not always known this. But who, now, was supposed to be looking at her, and why?'

The dreadful chapter went on to shift the questions from the author and into the consciousness of Blackeyes herself. Not once before in the narrative had the elderly male creator allowed the young female subject to ask herself a single question about her identity or her purpose, though it could be argued in his defence that all such enquiries of the self are of little practical value and if persisted with are merely one of the symptoms of mental derangement.

On this occasion, certainly, the questions snagged at the tight skein and began to unravel it. The lustre of her dark eyes became even deeper, even more of a barrier, as her inward attention took away her sight of the things in the room. A splash of silver made an elongated sliver on the carpet, and it slithered wider as the last of the cloud passed across the moon. In time, the pale shimmer touched her face, for she had not moved for several hours.

Blackeyes grieved, without words for the grief, like a swan with oil on its feathers.

Such mute suffering and dumb ignorance, visited upon the young woman with casual authority and elegant cruelty, maddened Jessica to the point of frenzy. Her teeth clacked hard against each other as she saw again the variety of ways by which Blackeyes had been given no mental volition: her thoughts, if they could be so described, were reduced even in the final crisis to the folding-in of a beautiful ring of petals. There was no possibility of seriousness. Blackeyes was a doll.

Jessica's eyes sought out Clementine. The childhood comforter seemed to stare back across the room at her, and the past murmured in the space between. Jessica looked away, compelling her attention back to the last few pages.

It was no good. She could dimly sense the stealthy approach of the same kind of torpor that had engulfed Blackeyes during the long hours of her last night on earth. Her will seemed to cower before it, like a creature creeping along without guide or landmark in a dank fog.

The neatly ordered words she had been re-reading and excoriating for the hundredth time began to blur and merge, and she felt herself compromising with them. Violent action or vigorous thought might break into the narcosis, but the heavy, drowsily melancholy acceptance stole a little deeper into her mind.

'Oh, Christ,' she half-spoke, forgetting that Christ was not a woman.

Echoing so vainly through the centuries – Kingsley had said, relishing the cadence – the two words spoken by Blackeyes had hung briefly in the air about her, and then disappeared without answer. Futility had swarmed in to fill the empty space. Each act she had ever done was drained of even its momentary significances. Her mind showed itself to her as nothing much more than an emptied nest at the top of a beautiful, shimmering tree that exposed the paler side of its leaves to the passing breeze. It was her body, only, which had been her being; her body, only, which had been the measure of value. Legs. Thighs. Belly. Breasts.

Blackeyes tried to recall what it had been like when she first sashayed down the runway, her heels clicking, the witty clothes whispering, the hand going to the jut of the hip as she swivelled, paused, sulkily glared, and returned, the object of every eye. She had thought, then, that they were looking at her, appreciating *her*: and what a powerful compensation it had been for all the prior times when she had felt a ghost in the room, a spirit in the streets, a person who did not know what to say, what to think, what to believe, or what the purposes of her body were.

Kingsley had not let her thoughts range back to any childhood experiences or any earlier aspirations, so that the final crisis in her life was made to seem an extension of the passivity which had characterized her working life. She had said so little in the text that there were no words plausible enough for her thoughts to express their anguish. She had disappeared, so to speak, while she was still there. Legs, thighs, belly, breasts, then nothing, nobody, no body.

The penultimate chapter gave her an apparently accidental glimpse of freedom, but only in order to hint at what-might-have-been and thus strengthen the pathos of the remaining pages. Cold winds whipped, billowed and plucked at her as, bent low like a jockey in a silver cap, she thundered the big German motorcycle along the winding country road. The air was bright, the speed exhilarating, the cold of no consequence, and delight surged within the blood as she felt the machine become a part of herself.

How she managed to get back to London in the studded, silvered and sex-signalling garb, and what exactly happened to the valuable motorcycle, was not explained. Perhaps she rode it all the way, flashed at by car drivers, hooted at by lorry men. Maybe she laid it down on its side, like a wounded Aryan god, in the yard in front of the railway station, and was then nudged and ogled along every mile of the track back to Victoria. Whatever she did, there was certainly a gap in Kingsley's narrative which was capable of being torn wider open.

Jessica had worked out most of the story that would go into the hole, even though she had by now acknowledged her inability to make it into words on a page. She stretched up on her toes to get down the wok from the top cupboard in her kitchen, poured in the oil, turned on the electric ring, and stir-fried her mind in a hiss and sizzle.

When the doorbell buzzed, she already had a smile on her face. It neither faltered nor widened as Uncle Maurice came into the room, and several minutes passed before she saw out of her own glaze that the old man was in considerable distress, babbling about thieves and stinking of whisky.

'Helpless,' she thought, still smiling. 'As helpless as a baby.'

28

This is what happened, if the smile is to be believed.

Blackeyes did not go back to her room. She did not lie on the sofa and submit to nothingness. She did not creep out before the cold dawn with only a dressing gown and shining boots over her nakedness, and slip so easily into the quiet and darkened park. The water in the Round Pond could not have swallowed up her knees and long thighs, or made a line around the naked swell of her belly. She was not to go without a ripple, leaving the pond to smooth itself flat and reflect back the sky.

Jessica said so, and she considered her word to be as good as Kingsley's.

Cold winds whipped, billowed and plucked at her as, bent low like a jockey in a silver cap, she thundered the big German motorcycle along the winding country road. The air was bright, the speed exhilarating, the cold of no consequence, and delight surged within the blood as she felt the machine become a part of herself. A wooden signpost of the old kind pointed the way to Maresfield, but there was another and narrower lane rising beside it, with skeletal hedges. She tugged the noisy monster around, and swooped up the hill, a Nicolette escaping from Kingsley's walled tower.

It was as well that she was going too fast to take proper note of the land hurtling past her, for now the hedges, trees and fields were not as bright with literary association, nor shifting in currents of adjectives. The old man knew nothing of this, and could not describe it.

Jessica's shelves showed that she read many types of book, some of them demanding, others stylish, and many argumentative. Even so, she still had an essentially vulgar mind, which is not so harsh a judgement as it might seem. 'The years in which she had been a model immersed her in the unwholesome and the trashy, where brightness was synonymous with artificial glitter and truth so far out of the question as to be no more than a distant star on a cloudy night,' Kingsley wrote, in magisterial excess, about Blackeyes. The same could be said about his niece. Jessica's education had been neglected, for her mother thought it more important to be 'feminine' (in the old use of the term) than 'qualified' (another ancient word), and her father was not really her father at all. The sort of private school for girls to which she was sent placed more emphasis on being ladylike than becoming human, and considered what it called Deportment to be an asset of greater value than any bookish accomplishment. The wonder was that she could read anything at all.

The consequence, however, was that as soon as Blackeyes rode the motorcycle out of Kingsley's penultimate chapter, she roared into a world made out of half-remembered women's magazine stories, half-ashamed yearnings, inadequately digested scraps of an opposing ideology, and an inability to describe emotion or landscape or motivation or speech or thought or anything else in original language.

Mind you, Jessica's amendments to the story suit me very well. I've edited out the most embarrassing and ill-composed bits, but otherwise left it alone:

*

Blackeyes was now going far too fast for a narrow road like this one. Zip-zip-zip went the hedges, flying past. Roar-roar-roar went the big motorcycle as it flung itself up the hill.

She remembered what it felt like to be gliding upwards on the garden swing at the house they had had in Buckinghamshire. The little girl had laughed and screamed and then lost her breath altogether, as the smiling face of her uncle swung close and then dipped beneath her.

Old pictures were in her head as the rush of cold air smacked at her face, but now there was no thrust in them, and no betrayal. This was good! Nobody could stop her, nobody could get to her. The world was no longer filled with cameras and cocks, bright lights and white powder, and lies, lies, lies. The crew way back behind her would have to pack up and go home. Pity that she hadn't run them down!

Oh, what a great bike. What fantastic speed. What power. And she was the rider, not for once the ridden.

Zip-zip-zip. Roar-roar-roar. Thundering into a long, climbing loop of what was now not much more than a rough lane with grass in the middle of it. She could not see the herd of fat, slow cows coming in the other direction, their tails swishing. They were being walked back to the milking sheds by an old herdsman who was almost as slow and almost as vacant as they were themselves.

As she straightened out of the worst of the loop, Blackeyes saw the cows, and at the same time realized that she was going to smash into them. They were straddled across the lane from hedge to hedge, and yards further back as well. A mess of blood and bone looked unavoidable, for the poor heavy-uddered beasts had nowhere to run.

Blackeyes opened her mouth to scream, but instead of letting the sound out and reverting back to the helpless condition she had been in no more than a quarter of an hour ago, she braked and twisted the motorbike at the same time, so that it reared up like a terrified stallion, swung itself inches clear of the first pair of ambling cows, and sprang at the small bump of grassy bank beneath the hedge at the nearest side of the lane.

She lost control at the same moment. The still roaring and clattering machine skidded sideways from under her thighs, and banged, bounced and hurtled in a terrible noise all along the hedge until it smacked hard down on a wooden gate and tumbled over the other side. Blackeyes went in the same direction, but not so far, and at a different angle. She flew through the air, too swift to make the smallest sounds of terror, straight over the topmost spikes of the hedge and into the field.

The cows, meanwhile, groaning in panic, and their milk-heavy udders slapping against their legs, went as fast as they could down the lane in the direction they had already been facing.

'Whoa!' shouted the hersdman. 'Whoa there! Whoa!'

He was not very bright, this old farm hand, and the shock of what he had just seen did not help him to think any better. Not knowing what to do about the accident, he let the priorities of his working lifetime take over, and went after the terrified cows, crying at them in a cracked voice.

A sound that Blackeyes could not hear. She was lying in the field like a broken toy, hands outstretched, face down, legs awkwardly twisted, and one little studded boot, one silver star from her breast, yards away in a ditch. Her silver helmet was still in place, and her ludicrously short skirt was torn open. Some crows had returned to the field after they had fluttered away during the noise of the accident, but because she did not move or make any sound, they ignored her. And there was nobody else to see.

The farmhouse which controlled these few fields was tucked away in a partly wooded fold on the other side of the disastrously winding lane. It looked as though it had been a much grander place many years ago, but although the house had a rather worn or even shabby air, so that you could not be quite sure at first glance where the living area ended and the first barn began, there was still something comfortable or even serene in the look of the farm. Across the muddied yard, for instance, was a pond, complete with ducks, and their sense of enjoyment seemed to spread way beyond their yellow beaks and busy waddles.

Still mooing and still trotting, the fat swaying on them, the black and white cows were coming up the boggy path which wound part of the way around the house, heading for the sheds. The old herdsman scurried after them, wielding his useless stick.

'Whoa, me beauties! Whoa there!' he was saying, without much conviction or urgency now, for they were going to the right place.

The young farmer who came out of the house, with half a slice of the bread he was eating in his hand, did not look pleased.

'Jack!' he called, the food still in his mouth. 'What the hell are you doing!'

161

'Getting them back in,' the herdsman said, flustered.

'You don't run cows full of milk! Have you gone raving mad!'

'They bolted!' Jack protested. 'They didn't half bloody go, the buggers.'

'But why? For God's sake, man, it's part of your job to – '

'Motorbikes. I bloody hates 'em!'

'Motorbikes?'

'Ar.'

But the farmer could see that Jack the herdsman, in his own slow and fuddled way, was furtively worried about something.

'Jack. What happened? What are you worried about?'

The herdsman looked at the cows and then at his employer. If he had been wearing a cap, he would have taken it off and scratched at his head.

'Her,' he said, ready to fidget.

'Who? What are you talking about – ?'

'Her on that bloody great bike, the loony.'

The young farmer felt as though he was coaxing information from a guilty child, but there was an anxiety on the herdsman's walnut of a face which made it absolutely certain to anyone who knew him that there was something seriously wrong.

'What about her? Come on, Jack! Out with it!'

'Her went up over that hedge like a – well, like a I don't know what – one hell of a cropper. But her didn't smack up against none of them cows, I'll give her that. Frightened them out of their wits, though.'

Jack looked at his boots as the younger man stared at him in bewildered alarm.

'She went over the – ? *What hedge?* Jack!'

'The one 'longside the field we used to call Ready Penny, when it was old Mr Teague's place – ay – her went over like a – I don't know what.'

'But was she hurt? Is she all right – ?'

Jack squinted at the barns, and seemed to be trying to see if he could put a reef knot into his tongue without bulging out his cheek.

'Don't expect so,' he acknowledged, reluctantly. 'Don't see as how her can be, the speed her were going. But them bloody cows took off like they were young 'uns, see, and I – '

He couldn't finish because he had been grabbed at each shoulder, and shaken hard enough to loosen his top plate.

'Didn't you check? Didn't you go and see if she was hurt or – or *killed* – !'

'I had to get them animals back to the shed, didn't I?' Jack protested, managing to be both ashamed and indignant. 'Of course I was going to go and have a look as soon as – '

His voice trailed away because he was talking to no one. The farmer had charged away without ceremony, scattering some ducks before scrabbling as fast as he could into an elderly and filthy Land-rover at the end of the yard. The car accelerated at such a mud-splay of a rate past Jack that the herdsman had to step back with more nimbleness than he had ever previously shown in his working hours.

The Land-Rover took the same lane at the same unwise speed as Blackeyes had done, and soon arrived alongside the expired motorcycle on the field side of the now damaged wooden gate.

Blackeyes was lying about twenty yards away, and she had not moved.

He thought at first, with a double gasp of breath, that this was someone or something thrown out of a flying saucer. The silver helmet glinted, the clothing was bizarre beyond human habit, and the torn-off star glittered under the hedge like an abandoned flake of the heavens: but in the same moment, and almost despite himself, his eyes fell on her long, slender legs, the line of her hip, the undulations . . .

He wondered for half a second whether he should attempt to move her, or simply put his jacket over her and race away into Maresfield for a doctor. He stooped beside the girl and saw that it was impossible to leave her without knowing whether she were dead or alive. And then she groaned.

Gingerly, he ran his hands over her, as though he dreaded that she would fall apart, and then gently turned her over. She opened her eyes and stared up at the sky, and then at him. His heart bumped.

'Blackeyes!' he said.

(You will understand, of course, that this and what follows is as much an embarrassment to me as if I had been caught whacking myself off in a room with closed curtains. Not too far behind Jessica's obtruding narrative, surely, are the echoes and seductive whispers of the kind of fiction she thinks she scorns, and affects never to have read.)

For a moment, they looked at each other. She did not seem to recognize him. He wondered whether she knew who she was herself, but he smiled at her, trying to be reassuring.

'I don't know whether you've broken anything, or – '

'Cows,' she said, in the faintest of murmurs.

'What?' he asked, straining to hear.

She did not answer, but a change of light in her eyes showed that she was immensely puzzled.

'Look at me,' he commanded, and held his hands around her silver helmet.

'The cows – ' she began, but her expression glazed a little, and slid away.

'No. Look at me!'

Her eyes continued to waver, darker tunnels in the dark, then cleared, and steadied. He let go of the helmet, and her head did not loll.

'Good girl,' he said, softly.

But then her expression seemed to recede behind a sheet of smoked glass again, so he held up his index finger in front of her.

'Look at my finger.'

She did not do so. He waggled it, and made her focus.

'What?' she said, and swallowed.

'Keep your eyes on my finger.'

He moved it from right to left, and on the second time her eyes followed.

'Good girl,' he said again, as quietly as before.

Blackeyes followed the passage of his finger once more, but as her eyes moved she let it go and settled her gaze on his face instead. He smiled at her, tentatively. Her eloquent, dark

164

eyes did not respond. He felt her examination of him go through to the bone, and a strong yearning rose up to meet it.

'I think you'll do,' he said, in neutral tones, and as though unaware that the phrase might have a wider application.

'Will I?'

'I mean – I don't think you've damaged yourself too badly.'

That's all you know, she thought. And, who are you? she thought. I know I know you, but . . .

'Are you in pain?' he was asking. 'Do you think you can stand up?'

She nodded, perhaps to both questions. At the movement of her neck, the certainty of who this man was came into her knowledge, as clearly and as physically as though he had walked into a room in her head, through a door opening with a current of air.

Using his forearm and then the dip of his shoulder as a prop, she began to haul herself to her feet, but her knees suddenly buckled, the field tilted out of true, and all the grey and green and brown around her merged into reddish haze. She said, 'oh!' in her throat, and fell against him. He turned the movement into a bigger one, scooping her up, easily, into his arms.

(Jessica implies, but does not go so far as to say, that there was an orchestra with a very assertive string section waiting none too patiently behind the hedge. My own feeling is that they began to play one of the numbers Blackeyes had distantly listened to at the wedding-cake of an hotel, on the evening she and the same man had walked along the cliff path.)

'Hey – ' she went to say, as the land swung more wildly and her head bumped, but then everything, all at once, decided to settle.

'I'll get you back to the house and fetch a doctor,' he said, trying not to be too conscious of the press of her silvered and leathered body against his chest. 'We can't see to you here, can we? And you're freezing cold!'

He carried her with a deliberately slow tread across the

slope of the field and through the broken gate. The crows waited for them to go, then returned to dig at the ground with their beaks, in the busy silence of undertakers. It was the birds in the hedge and in the tree opposite the gate which were singing.

So she said. So the lady said.

29

Alone in her bedroom in the middle of the night, the lovely lady sleeps, dreaming that she sits at a small white table in front of a smaller white page, looking too neat and too demure to have murder in her heart.

She had conjured up a chorus of birds, and found an Aucassin for the Nicolette walled up in the sleek stones of *Sugar Bush*, but her dream had its own logic, and the new ending still had to make more than a formal obeisance to the existing one.

Blackeyes had damaged her hands when she was thrown so violently over the hedge and into the field, and this satisfactorily accounted for the appearance of her bloodied fingers in earlier dreams and other versions. There still remained the naked body in the pond, with similarly torn hands and broken nails. Without Kingsley's last chapter, the inventions Jessica had already made would have no purpose, and the policeman she imagined into life would not be able to be the instrument of her vengeance.

There is a lot to pay back, said Blackeyes to Jessica, in Jessica's dream. Are you going to do it for me? Are you going to do it for yourself? The silent girl had become talkative.

'I used to be like that,' thought Jessica, still asleep.

Her dream swept on to incorporate the events of the few hours she had spent that night with the wreck of her uncle. He had arrived, in the taxi she sent, full of booze and self-pity, and although there was nothing unusual in such a combination, she had never before seen it in so disgusting a manner. She gave him a drink, and then another, and although his hands were covering his face every time she looked, he still managed to get the rim of the glass against his slack old lips. He was mumbling between the drinks, and on the third or fourth she distinctly heard the words 'teddy bear'.

'What about it?' she asked, abandoning any pretence of serving the food.

'The cunts,' he said.

'Who?'

'They stole it, Jessie. They took her away,' he cried. 'My little chickadee.'

He became too drunk to hold anything back. Several times she had to put her hand to her face to hold back the worst of the hilarity, and then, catching her, he had stamped indignantly to the door, only to fall down before he could reach it.

'Come on!' she said, still laughing. 'Get up, you old fool! Look what you've done. You've broken the leg of my chess table!'

'The cunts,' he said, tears on his cheek, making no effort to pull himself up.

Jessica tugged at his arm, but he refused to co-operate, moaning words of general abuse about the generation of locusts which had fallen upon the land. She left him to it, and moved behind the slatted blind where the Malayan chicken and the scooped-out pineapple lay wasting, in order to get herself a glass of mineral water.

Plop! plop! went his mouth as she came back to the middle of the room. He was fast asleep on the carpet. She stared down at him, and noticed that his flies were undone.

'You filthy old devil,' she said, amiably enough, and went to look out at the darkened mews, not sure what to do, or whether it was worth doing anything at all.

There was a light on in the house opposite, and it illuminated the sickly flop and straggle of plant death in the big white tubs on either side of the front door. The light thinned as it crossed the cobbles, and she thought she saw the shadow of a cat. Behind her, Kingsley snored and smacked his lips.

'Why don't you cut it off?'

The voice came from the corner of the room, with clarity, even though it was that of a small child. She had waited a long time for Clementine to speak, for the little one was her only witness, and Jessica had never been able to tell her mother what had happened because she knew that she would be punished, or

168

that some worse calamity would come leaping out at her at the turn of the stairs.

'You don't even have to unzip his flies,' the doll said.

Jessica did not turn from the window. She saw a dimmed reflection of herself in the glass, and part of the room hung suspended in its own reduced glow above the cobblestones of the mews. This is a picture in a dream, she said to herself. I am in the middle of a dream.

She tried to wake up, and the windows of the house opposite momentarily took on the shape of her bedside lamp, but when she studied it, waiting for her bedroom to reassemble itself, the windows had gone and she was facing into the living room once again.

Clementine sat on the end of the bookshelf, her chubby arms outstretched, the dimples on her cheeks taking the shadow.

'O My Darling, O My – ' Jessica started to hum, then stopped herself.

'My scissors are nowhere near sharp enough anyway,' she said to the doll, who hooded her blue eyes in disdain but made no other answer.

Kingsley opened his eyes, and frowned up at her.

This is not a picture in a dream, she said to herself. I am not in the middle of a dream. How could I have thought so, when every single thing is so perfectly clear? She could see the tufts in the carpet and the hairs in his nostrils, and when she looked at the back of her hand a fine trace of blue veins showed her the pulse of her own blood.

'Are you going to get up, Uncle?' she said, now that she was sure she was awake.

'Oh, Christ,' he groaned.

She stood above him for a while, contemplating him. He closed his eyes in a twitchy flutter, but they would not stay shut, so he sighed deeply, and found within himself his old literary boom.

'"So sad,"' he said, '"so strange, the days that are no more."'

Jessica drove her foot into his ribs, but her expression stayed as one in the calmness of contemplation, and did not distort.

169

'"Dear as remembered kisses after death,"' he sobbed, keeping the mannered boom in place even as his throat convulsed. '"And sweet as those by hopeless fancy feign'd."'

'Did you write that?' she asked, surprised.

'"On lips that are for others: deep as love,"' he moaned. '"Deep as first love, and wild with all regret."'

'Did you write that?'

The squint he sent up from the floor was full of contempt, and she felt her cheeks redden. No matter how much she read, she would never be able to catch up.

'"Deep,"' he boomed, with a glint of triumph in the tears at his eyes, '"as first love, and wild with all regret; O Death in Life, the days that are no more."'

'Yes,' she said, giving him another kick. 'Those are the ones I want to talk about.'

He moaned again, but she did not seem to have hurt him very much. I wonder if I should put on a different pair of shoes, she thought. She tried again, pulling her foot further back, and heard the bone crack as her toes thumped into his ribs.

'Tennyson,' he gasped, so she kicked him once more, in the same place.

After a little while, and a few more good blows into his side, her foot began to ache, right up to the ankle. He wasn't making any noise, let alone whiffling out one of his ancient verses, so she drank the remaining water in the bottle of Badoît and sliced up some cucumber to put on her eyelids.

'Tennyson,' she said to herself, stretching out on the sofa. Well, now, how many women poets had been silenced by the world in which they had been forced to live? Well, now, she sighed, making sure the cucumber slices did not slip. Well, now, isn't that right, isn't that the case?

'Indisputably,' she said out loud, separating the syllables, and easing her shoulders into the right position on the soft white leather. She glimpsed herself neat and demure in the white room, at last able to put the words on the white page.

How strange that it had seemed so difficult! It was true, then, that you could break out of the long oppression with a single act

170

of violence! The throb in her ankle faded to nothing as she saw the words coming out from beneath the clench of her hand, marching across the paper like an army of soldiers bearing their banners and halyards on high. Soldiers? What do I mean, *soldiers*? No, no, no.

30

An owl tawnily unaware of cliché hooted somewhere out in the early darkness of winter, perhaps in response to a scene that included glimpses of the cold, pale moon through tangles of black and bare branches. Smoke rose from the farmhouse chimney, flattened, and drifted away like wraiths about to be lost in the night. The bird looked around and about, and hooted again.

Blackeyes heard the sound, but was no longer in the mood to let such a mournful note sink down into her being. Much of the pain had seeped out of her bruised or grazed limbs, though her hands continued to hurt. She wrapped them round the steaming mug of soup, and sipped, and pondered, her legs tucked up on a deep but badly scuffed chesterfield in front of the fire. The logs fizzed and spat, half-way between anger and celebration, and she sipped again, pondered more, and looked with a wince at her torn fingernails. Habit made her go to groan about their condition – 'damaging the goods, darling' – but then she realized that, come what may, such things no longer mattered. Sod the job: damn the goods.

The young farmer came back into the room, bearing a basket of logs which he dumped down with a clatter on to the broad stone hearth. The fire did not seem to need feeding, but he squatted down in front of it, and handed the flames a few more knobbly rolls of wood.

'This place used to be full of elms,' he said, 'but of course they all went and died.'

He was putting the logs on the fire because, in this position, and doing something, he could appear perfectly natural while keeping his back to her. It was his face he worried about: emotions passed unedited and too quickly through its blood, skin and muscles, and the effort to hold them back frequently

172

subverted the signals. He suspected that the intense pleasure he felt at her presence in this old, flag-floored barn of a room would show itself as a wretchedly gleeful and hence compromising simper.

The last thing he wanted was a repeat performance of his encounter with her on the day she allowed him into her house. Neither his face nor his words had helped him out, and every attempt to break through the glassy shine of her skidded off into the ludicrous. He had wanted to feel like Schubert on holiday in Steyr, intoxicated by all the senses, but finished more like a slapstick comedian unable to get it up in a brothel. Not only did he turn down her apparently casual invitation or ultimatum to fuck or shut up, but he tried to get nearly the best of both by licking at her long neck and wide mouth in between a few longer and wider sentences. Before he went, he spilt cold tea over her and tried to wipe it off, giving himself an even more demanding erection in the process.

'I wouldn't mind – now – ' he had said, nodding at her bedroom door like a thief in pantomime, and unable to stop his nostrils quivering.

'Too late,' she said, and started to laugh, provoking him into a door-slam of a farewell, and a shouted expletive, which he was to hear in his head for many months after.

Within a fortnight, he had jacked in his job as a paid liar, cashed in a clutch of inherited equities, sold his unit trusts and his sports car, borrowed against his insurance policy, and one way and another, took half a share and the live-in interest in the farm he had so often persuaded himself he did not want. He did not know whether these events were connected, but, later, had begun to think that they were.

And now she was here! Wrapped up in his own dressing gown, looking at him, or at the fire, and it did not matter which. Both burned.

'Both burn,' he said to himself, wanting to laugh. 'Who's a damp twig, then?'

He brushed off his hands, and recoiled a little from the heat of

173

the blaze. Perhaps now was the time to see the trout leap above the water. He stood up, and turned.

'More soup?'

'No,' she said, and then remembered to add a thank-you.

'How do you feel?'

'Sore. But in one piece.'

'You know, you really were very lucky – '

'What, to meet a herd of cows?' she asked. 'Or to have you come along?'

He laughed and went to put his hand to his face, but stopped himself.

'I mean, you could have broken your neck. There are stones in that field. This was one hell of a neglected piece of land, I can tell you.'

She put the mug down, and looked at him, trying to remember his name.

'I – ' he said, and she waited, her expression still the same.

'Would you excuse me?' he said again. 'I'll be – I won't be more than twenty – '

He loped out of the room, before specifying seconds, minutes, hours or days. Blackeyes stared at the fire. Once, she had made up pictures in the movements of the flame and the shift of the fuel. She stared. What image was this, forming in the char of the wood and the dancing flickers? Did it come from the fire, or from her own head?

'No,' whispered her doubt. 'It cannot be. It can never be.'

But she got up, the dressing gown flapping around her, and told herself that she was curious about the room, rather than its owner. It reminded her of pictures of the parlour in the books she had been given to look at as a child. Here is the farmer with his horse and his cow. Here is the milk maid sitting on her stool. Here is the farmer's wife in the parlour . . .

Chick, chick, chick, little chicken
Lay a little egg for me.

She picked up a curved pipe from a cheap, plastic pipe-rack,

174

turned it in her hands, saw her broken nails again, and quickly put it back. A clock was slowly and heavily ticking out in the hall, but she couldn't see it.

'Where's the television?' she thought. 'Where's the record player?'

Restless, troubled by things she did not yet comprehend, Blackeyes moved to the window, which had such ill-fitting old frames that the curtains swayed in the draught. She pulled one of them aside, enough to look out, but it is difficult to see from a lighted room into the dark, and she let the curtain fall back.

She did not want to be left alone like this.

Her bones started to ache again, and her head throbbed. She wondered how many flagstones there were between the window and the chesterfield. One, two, three, four, five – no, begin again. Count something else. The triangles on the, on the . . .

'It's very old-fashioned but I've found you a night-dress – '

The plump, middle-aged woman coming in from the hall was the type to launch into speech as soon as she put foot in a room with somebody already in it. She was holding up a long, greyish-white billow of old silky stuff that might have been made from a redundant parachute at the end of the war.

'Miss?' she said, halting in mid-stride.

Blackeyes was standing in the middle of the room, swaying. Her eyes rolled towards the speaker, but could not hold.

The woman rushed towards her, dropping the night-gown, and held on to her. Blackeyes tensed, seemed about to protest, and then relaxed against the protecting grip.

'Oh, you poor skinny little thing! What are you doing? Come on, now, sit yourself down. You should have let the doctor see you, my girl. Come on! Get those feet up before they buckle under you!'

She led Blackeyes back to the chesterfield, making her lie down.

'I don't know about you. Riding nasty great motorbikes down a lane with cows coming along. And that Jack – ! Well. He wants a good butt ash around his backside, leaving you like that.'

175

'Jack?' Blackeyes asked, grabbing at a name.

'The herdsman, so called. Got no more up top than a cow hisself, that's the truth. You should see him eating his dinner! Just as though he's chewing the cud.'

Blackeyes, her head back against the scuffed leather, saw that the room had settled back into its former stillness. She heard most of the words, and steadied her gaze on the round little face that was so earnestly peering at her.

'What's his name?' she asked, abruptly.

'Who? Jack?'

'The man. The one who brought me into here – '

'Mr Richards, do you mean?'

Richards? But what was his first name? She could not get hold of it.

'Jeff,' the woman said, at the other's continued frown.

'You're not his mother, then?'

'Lord, no. I'm his housekeeper and chief bottlewasher.'

Blackeyes contemplated the fire, watched by puzzled eyes, then slowly shifted her dark gaze back again. It looked as though she were trying to work something out.

'Is he nice?' she asked.

'Nice? What's nice when it's at home? Why?'

'I don't know.'

The housekeeper seemed amused, and patted Blackeyes on the hand, until she saw the grazes, and the broken nails.

'Don't you think you'd be better off in bed, my dear?'

'So they say.'

'Sorry?'

'So they all say.'

Blackeyes was looking at the burning logs again, and her voice sounded remote, even cold. The older woman thought she understood what had been said.

'Never had that problem, myself. My poor old dad always used to say to me, ' "You'd better be good, my girl, for you can't be beautiful." '

The bleakness in Blackeyes as she stared, still, at the grate made the housekeeper's self-deprecating, and so, disguising

176

smile falter. She was glad to hear steps in the hall, and then the door opening.

'I'd forgotten all about the motorbike, so I went and fetched it,' Jeff said as he loped into the room, and pink from the cold outside, or something else.

'*Fuck the motorbike!*'

Blackeyes had swung her head and spoken like someone taking swift aim and firing a pistol. The housekeeper clapped her hand across her own mouth, as though she had let off the offending word. Jeff blinked, and straightened a little, obviously aware that some expletives are not in universal circulation.

'Never in all my born days – ' the older woman quavered.

'Now, now, Mrs Barnes,' Jeff interrupted, embarrassed.

'Oh, my dear. My dear,' Mrs Barnes said, taking hold of Blackeyes by the wrist so as not to hurt her fingers. 'It doesn't become you one little bit, not language from the gutter doesn't – '

'Mrs Barnes,' Jeff said, in a harder voice.

Blackeyes looked from one to the other, initially puzzled, then her forehead seemed to rise to meet her hair-line, and she said *oh, dear* in a tiny voice.

'Anyway,' Jeff said, with a flap of his arm, 'I've brought it back. It's not as badly damaged as I thought.'

'Thank you,' she said, but looking at Mrs Barnes, who let go of her wrist.

'I'm sorry, miss,' the housekeeper said, stiffly, and went out of the room, her head held at too rigid an angle. They heard her feet quicken into a run on the stone floor.

A log spat in the fireplace, but otherwise the room was silent.

'The last time Mrs Barnes went to the cinema, Clark Gable said "Frankly, my dear, I don't give a damn," or whatever it was that caused the huge fuss,' Jeff said, not sure whether he wanted to laugh or not.

The same log spat out a few more little stars.

'Listen,' he said. 'Hadn't I better telephone someone and let them know where you are – ?'

'No.'

'But – you can't simply sort of – disappear. Can you?'

She looked at him, and the thought that she could, that she might, came to her at the very moment she smiled. Disappear! Without trace! The smile widened until her teeth were showing.

31

Jessica did not rear up in her bed at the end of the bad dream, but lay still, her eyes half-open, and waited for the dread to recede back into all the familiar things around her. She had awoken at the place in her vengeful melodrama where her foot was hovering above Maurice James Kingsley's throat. At any moment, she was going to bring it down, hard, upon the loose grey scrag and Adam's apple, but then he had made a deep groan and opened one of his eyes.

'Sweet Jessie,' he croaked, a strange glow coming up towards her out of the single eye.

Sweet Jessie. Sweet, sweet Jessie. Sweet little, good little, pretty little baby. How well she remembered the words that he, presumably, thought she had forgotten. There was darkness at the windows, the new dolly was pressed tightly against her, and the far door was swinging open.

'Sweet Jessie,' he had said, leaning across on his knees, and kissing the top of her head. He had a snake with him which, mysteriously became a sticky part of his body, and he made her stroke it, pulling at her hand when she tried to stop. She both knew and did not know what was happening. In the end, the snake frothed at its single eye, or mouth, and she cried out in alarm. He put his hand over her mouth and wept himself until they were both silent. She could smell the tobacco on his fingers and then the sweat on his body, and the arm or the leg of the doll dug into the top of her leg.

Eventually, he had got back out of the car. She stayed where she was, trying to wipe her hands, and watching his dark shape walk a little way in front, and then stop. He did not move for a long time, but then he lifted his head and looked up at the sky, as though he were searching for the moon.

She picked up her doll, and held it tight. The movement

caused it to say *Ma-ma*, so she hushed it, suddenly so deeply afraid that she could feel ants, or something like, nibbling at the roots of her hair.

Uncle Maurice was still standing at the front of the car, his head tilted back. She wondered what was the matter with him. His face had stretched tight, his eyes had rolled white in the darkness, and she had seen the edge of his tongue flickering in and out of his mouth as he made the funny sounds.

'Clementine,' she whispered, looking into the china-blue eyes.

Was he going to come back? Was he going to stay there? She wanted to do wee-wees, but was too scared to get out of the car.

And then he fell over and she was standing above him, her foot hovering over his throat. Clementine was watching her from the corner of the room. Which room? I thought I was in bed. No, this is the living room. He was lying on his back on the carpet, looking up at her with only one of his eyes open.

'Sweet Jessie,' he said.

She stamped down as hard as she could on the exposed stretch of his throat, but the flesh seemed to be alive, and writhing. It was a snake that did not want to be crushed. Oh, but this was ridiculous! They were all over the floor, slipping, slithering and shining, and she had to clamp her teeth together so that she would not cry out and show how frightened she was. There seemed to be a nest of them coming out of the hole in his throat, but she kept bringing down the sharp heel of her shoe, and in the end they coiled back into the flesh.

Jessica realized that she had slipped back into sleep again, and that the same nightmare had reclaimed her. This time, she made herself sit up in the bed, in order to escape its serpentine insistences. She reached out for the drawer in the bedside table, but then closed it, and clicked on her lamp instead. No need to take another tablet. They didn't work anyway. 'Sugar and spice and all things nice,' she wanted to say to herself, for no apparent reason.

She threw back the bedclothes, and put her feet to the floor. Why did I go to sleep in my clothes, she wondered, irritated at herself. She looked at the little clock on the bedside table, and saw that it was only half-past three in the morning. Sure enough, the thin chime came in old silver from across the roof-tops.

Her shoes lay next to the pine chest of drawers, one upright on its slender heel, and the other next to it on its side. They reminded her of two small but graceful animals, a mated pair, one asleep and the stronger one standing guard. Then she noticed the mess on the heel, and shuddered so much that a wave from her stomach threw something against the wall of her throat.

The living room was dark when she reached it in a rush of her bare feet. Her hand trembled so much that she needed two plunges at the switch on the wall to get the lights on.

Maurice James Kingsley lay on the carpet, his eyes open, and his throat smashed to a pulpy slick of blood and sinew. Strangely, the sight of him calmed her at once. She stood looking down at the old man, and there were no tremors moving across her skin.

'Crikey,' she said, and almost, but not quite, wanted to laugh. After all, it had been years since she had used such a word. A games mistress loomed across the net, wobbling with indignation, accusing her of deliberately hitting the ball at the other girl when she was not ready to receive. Quite so, Miss Truelove.

Jessica saw that the blinds were open at the window, and wondered how dangerous that might be at this time of the night. She looked out upon the dark mews, the white tubs, the yellow door, and the windows of the house opposite. All was quiet. But then she jumped inside as she thought she saw a movement at the window. It could have been the shape of someone withdrawing into the denser blackness of the room.

Careful! Be careful! hissed her head.

She closed the blinds, and returned to the body. Perhaps a drink would be a good idea. In the kitchen, though, the vodka bottle was empty, and there was no mineral water left in the fridge. Do everything slowly, she said to herself as she ran the tap. Why? So that it can be written down. She drank the water, and put the glass on the kitchen work-top. Will there be wipe-clean surfaces in heaven? she asked herself. Of course not. All the theologians were men, and what did they care?

Men, men, men, murmured her mind, as she took down the copy of *Sugar Bush* from the shelf. Men, men, men, it repeated as she tore the margins of the pages into thin strips of white paper. She sat at the table, so neat, so demure, and shuffled through the strips until she found the one she considered to be the most suitable.

Upon this, she began to write a list of names in the tiniest letters she could manage. Men, men, men. As each one came back to her, clawing so eagerly at her clothes and at her body, she pinioned his name to the strip of paper. When she had finished, after letting the occasional one escape, she let her eyes swivel to the metal-stemmed mirror she kept at the edge of the table.

'Maurice James Kingsley,' she intoned in a rehearsed and theatrical resonance, 'took if for granted that sleep and torment were natural partners – '

Twisting in her chair, she turned to look at him. He was so repellent, lying there, that nausea rose in her, and she had to force herself to reduce him back into words: an object in his own story as amended, in justice, or even with a certain amount of literary criticism, by what he would have called her own fair hand.

It was with the same clarity of purpose that she took hold of his ankles and dragged him out of the room. Everything she had striven to work out was now falling into place, as properly as punctuation marks.

The back-yard – called a patio by the estate agents who sold the mews house to her – boasted an oblong of tired earth at the end of the slabs which mostly covered it. She had already measured the stretch of soil with her eye, and knew that it was just about big enough to take the old man. Her inventions even allowed for the hardness of the earth below its damp top layer. She worked her hands as a burrowing animal might, scooping the dirt behind her. Some of it fell across the body she had pushed, dragged and rolled for the last few yards of its journey.

Her nails soon split and broke with the digging, and by the time she had made a big enough trench, her fingers were bleeding as well.

High walls and darkness protected her, although they could not muffle the gasps of effort as she pulled Kingsley to the edge of his grave, and pushed him in. She looked down at him, letting her breathing return to normal, and felt a residual pang of what might have been compassion. A man of letters needed at least a few lines of verse as a suitable valediction, but Jessica could not remember any. Also, she was getting cold.

Wait a minute. There *was* something. How did it go?

> If I should die, think only this of me:
> That there's some corner of a foreign field
> That is forever England.

She did not succeed in getting the words in the right order, and accepted that they were not in any case entirely fitting, but she overcame both these difficulties (as well as a spasm of giggles) by dutifully intoning what she took to be a masculine and funereal drivel in the right sort of voice.

'There,' she said, in her own brisk direction. 'That's done.'

She swept the loose dirt on the slabs back into the hole with a hard broom, happy to recognize and make use of the symbol of abused sisterhood. Some of it scattered across Kingsley, but what did he care? The big mound of earth was left until the last.

Jessica was exhausted. Rewriting was painful, and now she had stepped across the barrier into genuine first-order creation. She propped the broom up against the back wall, took some deep breaths, and then looked up at the sky, wanting to see the stars. But London had thrown up a misty blanket to protect itself from a vastness which so greatly exceeded its own. Perhaps one of Maurice James Kingsley's former Occasional Pieces could have explained to her why the city so often cowered in this way after dark, for he had at many times composed sententiously prattling little essays on the theme of 'nocturnal urban moods', but he was no longer in a condition to eructate such words into the market place.

A long, thunder-like rumble overhead reminded her that the first flights from North America were on their way into Heathrow, and she must make haste. She took off her muddied dress and threw it into the shallow grave. Now, only flimsy underwear rode upon her beautiful limbs, and she was reminded of her former occupation. In mockery, she walked the length of the yard in an exaggerated wiggle, turned, splayed out and undulated her arms, and walked back again. She had forgotten that there was still a man left to see this performance: me.

Jessica took off her underclothes and threw them into the hole. Her silky little panties, the last to go, fell across Kingsley's face in an irony she had not so precisely intended, but which I certainly did.

Naked now, yet no longer cold, Jessica pushed the mound of earth into the trench, then patted it down with her hands and her feet. All that remained for her to do was to go back upstairs, insert the carefully rolled list of men's names into a little waterproof pouch, and the pouch into herself, put on her short, shining boots and a dressing gown with a paperclip in the pocket, then flit through a few dark and deserted streets to the railings of Kensington Gardens.

Once she had got into the empty park, it was a small matter to discard the wrap, fold it neatly beneath a dripping tree, and walk in an absolutely straight line across the already trampled grass and into the Round Pond. The clock on the palace silvered the quarter again, and she wondered if the princess were awake.

In next to no time, there was nothing but her head to be seen, then a few strands of floating black hair, and soon she was completely submerged, with no sign of fuss or struggle. The water smoothed itself flat, and reflected back the sky. There could be no doubt, though, that Jessica had removed a crucial sentence from Maurice James Kingsley's last paragraph.

As her lungs filled, she had the satisfaction of knowing that Blackeyes was free. Well, sort of free, anyway, for it is me that is waiting outside her door, ready to claim her.